WORLD LITERATURE IN TRANSLATION

LI CUNBAO

THE WREATH
AT THE FOOT OF
THE MOUNTAIN

Translated from the Chinese by
CHEN HANMING
and
JAMES O. BELCHER

GARLAND PUBLISHING, INC.
NEW YORK & LONDON 1991

Library of Congress Cataloging-in-Publication Data

Li, Ts'un-pao.
    [Kao shan hsia ti hua huan. English]
    The wreath at the foot of the mountain / by Li Cunbao ; translated by
Chen Hanming and James O. Belcher.
        p. cm.—(world literature in translation ; v. 6)
    Translation of: Kao shan hsia ti hua huan.
    ISBN 0-8240-2992-5
    1. Sino-Vietnamese Conflict 1979—Fiction. I. Title. II. Series.
    PL2877.T74K3413   1990
    895.1'352—dc20   90-3019

Printed on acid-free, 250-year-life paper
Manufactured in the United States of America

THE WREATH
AT THE FOOT OF
THE MOUNTAIN

ख़

I can't remember which poet of which dynasty of which era wrote these immortal lines: "Inferior as I am, I dare not forget to concern myself with the destiny of the country."

Preface

It was at the headquarters of the Third Battalion of some infantry regiment on Ailao Mountain that I first met Zhao Mengsheng, the protagonist of my story. Zhao was the battalion's political instructor. Born into a revolutionary family, Zhao's father is an old general with an illustrious military record. His mother also is a veteran, serving in the Eighth Route Army. Zhao himself was awarded a first-class merit in the fight against Vietnamese invaders three years ago. Since then, he has abandoned the comforts of big city living, and has stuck to his post on the border in Yunnan Province. What's more, he talked his wife, Liu Lan, into leaving the big city to come and serve as an army surgeon at this border outpost.

This much information had been given to me by a clerk in the Corps Cultural Institute before I met Zhao. The clerk added, "It's not going to be easy to interview Zhao Mengsheng. The man's an eccentric. He's been decorated for bravery, but his name's never been in the newspapers because he always turns down interviews."

An eccentric? Maybe a man of character. Anyway, he sounded like just the sort of person a writer would like to meet.

Seeing that I was going to insist on meeting Zhao, the clerk phoned the regimental political department. But after calling, he again tried to talk me out of going: "Come on, Li; you'll end up going there for nothing. They said Zhao got a money order for 1,200 yuan from up your way—somewhere around Yimeng Mountain in Shandong province—a couple of days ago and he hasn't slept for two nights."

Now, how could a money order upset the stalwart son of a general? There was a story in this, all right. I set out without giving it a second thought.

When I finally saw Zhao in person, he tried to brush me off by saying, "Nothing to tell." The secretary in battalion headquarters, Duan Yuguo, who was seated with us, tried to conceal the awkwardness of the situation by getting up to pour more water into my already full teacup. Zhao remained silent. He was handsome and trim, fit to be an honor guard. And although his eyes were bright and his eyebrows dashing, a deep grief and sorrow nevertheless clouded his eyes, a state that sleeplessness alone could not account for. Could this be the result of a money order?

Zhao seemed to be oppressed by boredom, too, and took off his cap for no apparent reason. I immediately noticed a scar two fingers wide high upon the right side of his forehead. While I searched my mind for some conversation to lift the tedium, he quite unexpectedly began to speak: "You must be from Shandong, I suppose, from your accent."

"Yes, that's right. My hometown is near Yimeng Mountain."

"You work in the Jinan Command?"

"Yeah, I'm a writer in the art troupe."

"Then what are you doing in Yunnan?"

I told him that I had been transferred along with the infantry to Yunnan early in the spring three years ago. The fighting there had attracted worldwide attention, and now I was writing a follow-up series on how the combat heroes I'd interviewed then were doing today.

"Oh." He nodded out of politeness.

I decided I had better make my move. I said, "Instructor Zhao, would you tell me how you talked Liu Lan into coming to this border post?"

"What! You expect me to brag about Liu Lan? And make a fool of myself?" He shook his head repeatedly, and said sarcastically, "Oh, well, she's gone home to visit her family—and has been absent without leave for over twenty days! We were just talking about taking disciplinary action, isn't that right, Xiao Duan?"

The secretary, Duan Yuguo, looked to be about twenty-four years old, pasty-faced and intellectual. He answered earnestly, "Yes. Dr. Liu has overstayed her leave by twenty-two days. However, she has a doctor's note for sick leave."

"A note! Now, if that isn't a cheap trick," Zhao said to me with indignation. "After she graduated from the Military Medical College, she did get assigned to this place. But before the year was up she

2

started asking to get transferred to civilian work. She said the life here wasn't fit for a human being. There's probably no power on earth that could keep her here on the border."

After he finished his speech, he fell deep into his own thoughts again.

It was March and we had just gotten more snow when I left Jinan, but down in the subtropics of lower Yunnan, the weather was sweltering. The shrill chirping of the cicadas outside the window made the dry heat even worse. I had just decided that this interview was going nowhere when Zhao began to talk.

"Since you've come down from Shandong, I'd like for you to have a look at this."

What he handed me was the money order for 1,200 yuan! It was drawn at the Date Blossom Valley Production Brigade Station, Yimeng Mountain Region, Shandong Province. A short note attached to it read—

> Mengsheng, this is the money you've been sending to your Aunt Liang over the past three years. Now we're returning it all to you. Please cash it.

"It got here the day before yesterday. I don't see a single reason for Aunt Liang to return the money!" He hit his head with his fist. His face twitched in agony.

There was a long silence. After he had calmed himself, he said, "I had an extraordinary experience both before and after the battle. That could be why I've stayed here at the frontier till now." He paused, and then looked at me squarely. "I would like to tell you all about it, if you're interested."

I nodded several times. "Sure, please go ahead."

He stood up from the chair. "First I would like to show you these two photos."

I hadn't noticed the two framed photographs hanging on the wall above his desk. Zhao pointed to the one on the left and said, "This enlarged photo is a portrait of the main character in the story I'm going to tell you. His name was Liang Sanxi. He was from Yimeng Mountain, Shandong Province. He was commander of Company Nine, Third Battalion. He sacrificed his life in the battle. I was political instructor with Company Nine then."

Before I had time to get a close look at the photo of the commander, Zhao turned to the larger picture on the right. "This is the whole family of the martyr, Liang Sanxi. This photo was taken in front of his grave. The old woman with the patches on her clothes is Aunt Liang, his mother. The young woman in mourning is Liang's wife, Han Yuxiu. In her arms is Panpan, the daughter that Liang never saw."

We both sat back down. Zhao was still depressed.

I took a portable tape recorder out of my knapsack and quietly loaded a cassette. Zhao suddenly stopped me, saying, "Wait a minute. Before I tell you anything, I have three conditions that you're going to have to agree to."

"What are they?" I asked quietly.

"First: when you write down *my* story for your readers, don't try to decorate the truth with fancy words. It's got to stay true to the everyday life of army troops. A literary work ought to have its own inherent value; anyway, isn't honesty itself a kind of beauty?"

I was surprised to find a political instructor who knew anything at all about literature; yet, what he said was all a professional writer would say. I nodded to him in approval.

"Second: readers aren't very much interested in war stories anymore. In my opinion, this is because military themes have become too unrealistic. There is no real conflict and, therefore, little appeal to the reader. The Russian critic Belinsky said that a novel without dramatic action is dull and insipid. It's true. And then some writers just invent potboilers to dress up their dramatic effects, which makes their novels all the more unbelievable. But rest assured, my own experience has been dramatic enough. You will, I expect, feel a little bit bored when I start to narrate. I beg you to listen with patience, and I hope you won't interrupt me. In the end, you'll agree that the real-life story I'm going to tell you could touch the heart of a statue and make it shed tears." He stopped talking, and looked at me. "Can you write it down without the whitewash?"

I nodded again.

"Third: both my mother and I played negative roles in the story. You must describe my behavior strictly according to the facts; in other words, if you glamorize my deeds even a little, your story will end up either dull or unbelievable. So the third condition is the most important one."

I was puzzled.

Then Secretary Duan said to me, "In the story that our instructor is going to tell you, I played a negative role too; and I sincerely hope that you show no mercy on me."

I was even more puzzled.

"Three conditions, then—especially the third one. Can you accept them?" Zhao was insistent.

I was more than ready to hear him out, and quickly nodded agreement.

The following is Zhao's story.

One

It was September 6, 1978. The date stands out in my mind because that was when I transferred from the corps publicity department to be a political instructor in Company Nine. My life as a photographer in publicity might have seemed free and easy. The truth is, I never was much more than an amateur at photography, and I didn't get along with the others, who were only too happy to see me leave.

Everything I owned had been sent ahead to Company Nine by the regiment's logistics department two days before I arrived. The regiment's jeep carried me and my personal baggage to my new post. The only thing I had carried with me that was worth anything was one carton of Chunghwa Cigarettes and a Yashika camera. I'd had to turn in my work camera, so my mother had asked somebody to buy the Yashika for me in an import shop while I was home on vacation the previous August. Now, I could still dabble in photography with my Yashika.

I first met Liang Sanxi and the platoon leaders of Company Nine at their camp, which was at least a thousand li from this border outpost. It was also in an uninhabited mountain area. Liang clasped my hand very enthusiastically. "Welcome! Welcome to our company! It's been over half a year since Instructor Wang left for military school. We've been waiting for a new instructor for months."

Liang was a big man, at least two centimeters taller than my 1.77 meters. His swarthy face was thin but square. His thick, tight lips showed an honest, good nature; his chin pointed upward a bit. You could see that he had joined the army with hay seeds in his hair.

He looked me over. "You must be twenty-six or seven, I'll bet."

"I'm not young anymore. I'm thirty-one," I said.

"Then we're the same age—the year of the pig." He smiled. "But you look at least seven or eight years younger than me."

"So you've learned how to flatter people by lowering their age, Commander," a platoon leader standing beside me said to Liang. He gave a comical smile. "Well, one dark face and one light one. You two pigs will still be eating out of the same trough."

Liang Sanxi introduced the artillery platoon leader to me as "the company buffoon."

"Jin Kailai . . . Jin Kailai," the artillery platoon leader said, repeating himself as he shook my hand. "And not a buffoon, but the greatest complainer in the whole regiment."

Liang then introduced the other three platoon leaders one by one.

Liang Sanxi, looking much older than me, smiled honestly: "All right. You're in charge of the civilian work, and I'm the military. Let's work together." After a moment, he sighed. "The vice-commander joined the training corps and the vice-political instructor went home to visit his wife in the hospital. That left only these four guys and me to do all the work. I'm glad you're here; otherwise, I'd never get to take any leave this year." Jin Kailai interrupted him. "Commander, you'd better apply for leave tomorrow and go home next week. You can't keep putting Han Yuxiu off. She's expecting any day now." Then he turned to me. "Damn it all. Junior officers are as bad as monks." My new partners didn't seem to be too big on fancy words. I liked that.

A bugler sounded the call to emergency muster. The scurry of footsteps told me that it was time for me to be sworn in.

"Comrades," Liang said earnestly, introducing me to the whole company, "this is our new political instructor, Instructor Zhao." After thunderous applause, the ranks became quiet again. I had been to a few outfits to take pictures of the troops when I was a photographer in the publicity department, but I had never before seen ranks as disciplined as these. The four ranks were like four ruled lines. Each man stood bolt upright. An outfit is the mirror of its commander. Liang must be the type that makes his troops toe the line.

"Comrades, Instructor Zhao asked to come here from the corps' institute, *voluntarily*. He is a man of letters." Then his mild tone changed completely, and he scrutinized the ranks assembled in front of him. "Comrades, don't make the mistake of thinking that Instructor Zhao came down here as a temporary, just to get some experience. He is the official political instructor of Company Nine. All of his gear and his Party membership credentials came along with him. From now on, you ask him for instructions and you send in your reports to him. A soldier obeys orders—and you obey *his* orders. Now, let's ask our instructor out here to make a speech." Applause again. Great guys. They did everything as if they were mounting a bayonet assault, even clapping their hands.

"Comrades, I . . . I'm afraid I'm pretty much a greenhorn. I . . . I'll work with you for the good of our company. I . . . that's all."

I used to be a man who never had any trouble speaking confidently. And yet, under the ready gaze of the troops, my "inaugural address" ended up being very brief. I could still feel my cheeks burning and my heart pounding after Liang dismissed the troops. Playacting. I was playacting. But what kind of a play was it? A comedy? Horseplay? Or maybe a real tragedy. The political representative is the Party's man. I felt like I was desecrating the position.

Some school graduates join the army in order to get a decent job after their discharge. It's called "curvilinear employment." When I applied for a transfer from the institute to Company Nine, it was a "curvilinear transfer" trick.

I was born into a military family. When they instituted military rank, my father was made a major general and my mother a lieutenant colonel. I remember quarreling once with another boy over whose father held the highest rank. We got into a scuffle.

"You're just trying to show off, Zhao Mengsheng. Your dad only has one bean on his collar ensign. My dad has four!"

"That doesn't mean anything," I answered back. "My dad's bean is gold, for a general. Your dad's four beans are silver, for a colonel. Silver ones aren't the same as a gold one."

"You're just a braggart!"

"Is that so? You go ask your dad about it. If my dad told him to stand at attention, he wouldn't dare stand at ease."

A few punches and kicks, and then we were locked in a fight. Later, when my father found out about it, I got a good beating. I had never seen my father so angry. I wailed and threw myself into my mother's arms like a spoiled child. But Mother pushed me away and scolded me: "What does anybody's rank matter? We are all servants of the people. Never forget that you are a descendant of the Red Army, and you must serve the people when you grow up."

Back then, my parents were very strict with me. They never let me ride in the automobile that was allotted to them, and I had to wear clothes that my sister had outgrown. Mother often told me of the hard life during the war years, and the stories of heroes. She made a point of buying me picture books about the heroes. Following their example, my friends and I learned to love helping others. In the mornings, we helped crippled classmates to school. After school, we helped the dependents of soldiers and revolutionary martyrs buy rice and flour from the grain shop. During the winter, we helped the school custodian light the stoves in the classrooms. Each summer our teacher used to take us out of the city on camping trips. We would sit around the camp fire and dream about the heroes and our own bright futures.

Then military rank was abolished in 1965. My happy, carefree childhood became chaotic. By the time I joined the army, in 1967, Father had been taken into custody. After many requests, Mother agreed to take me to see him. She told him quietly, "Now Mengsheng has some prospects at last. He enlisted in the army."

Father stretched his arms through the iron bars to caress my cheeks with trembling fingers. "No tears, my child. A soldier never sheds tears lightly. All right, steel yourself in gunfire. Bear in mind why you were named Mengsheng—because you are a son of Yimeng Mountain, and you are the son of a soldier."

I came to this corps, which had gone down south from Shandong Province during the War of Liberation. Many of the officers in the corps, division, and regiment ranks had been my father's subordinates. I was moved to tears by the generosity of those career soldiers who, when Father suffered his misfortune, honored their years of friendship with him by taking good care of me.

The social and political turmoil of the next ten years ruined so many talents, yet the scramble for power and personal gain made so many people begin to see the light. Of all the creatures in the universe, humans are the cleverest and the most adaptive. Drawn into the life-and-death political maelstrom, the kindhearted turned cruel; the honest, deceitful; the thoughtful, superficial; the gentle, violent. It was as if by a single command, *"Change,"* the Creator had reversed everything.

All of us, regardless of our rank, have an ability to adapt. Although a vice-minister in the military regional public health ministry, my mother somehow developed a talent for social interaction, just like a diplomat. This had already started before Lin Biao—the greatest dissembler in the history of Chinese civilization—died in a plane crash. After that event, Father was reinstated in the army at his previous rank. Then, Mother brought her talent for diplomacy into full play.

Mother's diplomatic capabilities touched upon all matters, important and trivial. She would get scarce medicines or tonics for her comrades-in-arms. Using the long-distance phone lines, she would do whatever it took to arrange for travel so her colleagues could "recuperate" from vague illnesses, whether it meant going from north to south in winter or from south to north in summer like the seasonal migrations of birds. However, Mother was at her "diplomatic" best when it came to enrolling her associates' daughters in the army. In those days, parents in the cities shouted Chairman Mao's axiom, "The countryside is a vast world that provides wide enough scope for your abilities"; but all the while they worked to get better careers for their children—especially their daughters—by any means available to them. Every girl, well-connected or not, long dreamed of being a career soldier. My elder sister actually passed the examinations and enlisted in the Shanghai Army Medical University in 1962; Mother didn't need to waste any diplomacy on her. My two younger sisters donned army uniforms on the same day, and we became known as "the whole family bearing arms."

People raised their eyebrows behind Mother's back and whispered references to the "Red Detachment of Women." But they greatly exaggerated the number. I knew very well that Mother only signed up a dozen or so girls into the army, which was a "Squad of Women" at most.

"Is it against the law to send girls into the army? It's their right and duty to defend our homeland," Mother often asserted in her own defense. "The Polar Bear prowls our borders spoiling for a fight, and being a soldier means being ready for the shedding of blood. You'll see Zhao's whole family bearing arms when the war breaks out."

I never believed that those words came from the bottom of her heart, of course; still, I was very proud of being kept under Mother's mighty shelter. That is why it came as a surprise when she met with difficulties in sending my wife, Liu Lan, to the university.

In the summer of 1977, S Army Medical University decided to enroll two students from our corps. The applicants had to have recommendations and also pass an examination. Liu Lan was then working in the corps' outpatient clinic, and Mother, through her greatest efforts, had just gotten Liu promoted from nurse to assistant doctor. Soon, Liu Lan started to imagine that she was a student in the medical university. Mother made one long-distance call to recommend her, and as a result, Liu Lan was admitted, even though her marks were third from the bottom of twenty examinees. Or course, the other girls were outraged to realize that they had gotten short shrift. They launched a letter-writing campaign near and far to expose the fact that Liu Lan not only had been promoted, but had also been admitted to the university through her "back door" connections. They complained, in no uncertain terms, that the winners had been selected not according to their talent and knowledge but rather as a result of their power and social status. One of them even demanded a fact-finding panel to uncover the inside story and disqualify Liu Lan for university study.

As soon as she received my call for help, Mother came to our corps at top speed, like Kissinger shuttling to and fro in the Middle East. She was very upset when I described the situation to her, but soon she calmed down. She took me to visit two of my father's former subordinates.

"Does anyone think it's easy for us veterans to survive the turmoil of this Cultural Revolution?" Mother said to one of them. "Somebody seems to think that Mengsheng's father and I have not suffered enough. Whoever it is seems to be making us the target of their attack. If the rank and file have complaints against me, I'll let you straighten them out. I won't interfere in Liu Lan's affairs. I leave it to your discretion." When it was time to leave, Mother smiled to the officer and said, "Oh, I forgot to tell you. Your third son is showing superior abilities at our regional headquarters, and he has gained a high reputation. I have heard he is to be promoted to vice-section chief."

Later, she said to the other of Father's former subordinates, "It's true that Liu Lan's marks were a bit lower. But that was due to the ten years of turmoil. Her parents are both local cadres. It would take three days and three nights to tell you the tortures they suffered a few years ago. The upshot is that Liu Lan's low marks are the direct result of the poor education she received during the turmoil, and that's why she should study at the university. How can she serve the people well without adequate skills? You leaders should explain this fact to the comrades." As she was leaving, Mother shook his hand and said, "Oh, I almost forgot to tell you the good news: your fourth daughter is showing great promise in the second department of internal medicine at our general hospital. She was admitted into the Party a few days ago. Oh, yes, and she's old enough for a proper match now. What a concern children are for us parents! Rest assured, though, that I'll watch over her as if she were my own niece."

Mother accomplished all this through what appeared to be idle conversation. She did not need to make naked deals like a vulgar go-between, nor to drive hard bargains like a peddler. But there was no misunderstanding Mother's unspoken message: diplomatic interaction has to be carried out among equals; courtesy demands reciprocity.

Liu Lan's situation finally quieted down. If we hadn't pursued Liu Lan's promotion to assistant doctor, she and I would have both been transferred to my parents' protection. As it was, now that Liu Lan had entered the university, my own transfer was next on Mother's agenda.

In a stroke of good fortune, Corps Commander Lei, whom we referred to as Thunder God in a pun on his name, was reinstated after being stripped of his rank for ten years. I was delighted at his return, especially since Mother had told me that she had saved Thunder God's life during the War of Resistance against Japanese Aggression. One nod of approval from Thunder God and I could swing out of the corps and back to my parents' watchful protection without any problem.

Unfortunately, as soon as he returned to the corps, Thunder God flashed fierce bolts of lightning. He began the "rectification of incorrect styles of work" in the Party committee and the corps institute. He wouldn't bother to spare anyone's feelings, even his own parents'.

It used to be rare for officers of less-than-regimental rank to get transferred from one military region to another. But now, even ordinary soldiers can get those transfers. An officer of company rank, such as a political instructor, only needs the approval of his division to be transferred to another military area. Earlier, of course, it would have been a flagrant violation. Anyway, someone suggested to Mother over the telephone that to leave the corps I would first need to leave the institute of the corps, and not do anything illegal right in front of Thunder God's eyes.

I learned through the personnel department roster that the position of political instructor for Company Nine was open. As a result of that and my backdoor connections, I was officially named to the post.

The company commander, Liang Sanxi, was completely in the dark about the whole story. After lunch together, he showed me around the barracks. We inspected the company's vegetable gardens, the pig farm, and tofu production unit, each stop illuminated by his commentary. As soon as he had set up afternoon military training for each of the platoons, we went back to company headquarters where he gave me information on the company's ideological work.

Liang Sanxi had actually accepted me as a political instructor who would take root in Company Nine. As we sat, face to face, he spoke in a soft voice. I took notes pretending to be interested, a role that was not easy to play. I wondered how this "curvilinear transfer" would end.

Two

Taps sounded. Liang Sanxi and I lay on our beds, separated by a desk. He had told me that tomorrow morning the exercise would consist of a "full-dress, ten-kilometer cross-country march." He said that since I had just arrived from a desk job, it would be a while before I got used to the intensity of life in a field unit. He said I could leave my field pack behind and only bring along my pistol for the march.

Company Nine was the advance outfit for the whole regiment in military training. I had no idea how hard the work would be for the infantry unit in charge of military training. The troops in production or even those digging tunnels worked less arduously. I was quite unprepared mentally to bear such hardships.

I was sleeping soundly when I felt someone shaking me. I recognized Liang Sanxi's voice. "Hurry, Instructor, the bugle is sounding."

I got up hastily. Still drowsy, I pulled on my uniform. It was too late to pack my kit. Without buttoning up my coat, I rushed out of the company headquarters, pistol in hand. I had done my level best, and judged myself to be moving along quickly enough. But by the time I hurried up to the assembly point, Liang Sanxi had led the fully equipped and armed soldiers away.

"Instructor, Commander asked me to wait for you here," said the bugler, Jin Xiaozhu, in a child's tinny voice. As he ran ahead, he turned and called to me. "Hurry, Instructor, I know the way."

It was pitch dark. The morning star still shone in the sky. The rugged, winding mountain path stretched out in front of us. Feeling my way in the dark, I ran and ran. A sudden stumble threw me down.

Though fully equipped and armed, Xiao Jin had to turn back to help me get back up.

I had gained a reputation for lassitude around the corps institute. Someone even started a joke about my sleeping late every morning, saying that I was "Number One Sleeping Dragon." I never made it to the dining room in time for breakfast. Liu Lan had reminded me time and again—from the point of view of nutrition—that breakfast was extremely important. Well, it happens that I had read about how many calories the human body needs, and I was not going to let myself fall short. Every morning, after a good night's sleep, I would get up and have first a glass of thick orange juice and then two pieces of delicious chocolate or cake. Really! How could I, "Number One Sleeping Dragon," suffer rude hardships? But to keep up a good front, I had to grit my teeth and tough it out.

I followed the bugler, Xiao Jin, up the mountain and was soon out of breath. By the time we had climbed halfway uphill, still far from the top, we met Liang Sanxi leading the rest of the company back. He stopped in front of me and whispered, "Two minutes faster to the top than the last cross-country march."

I was so soaked with sweat that I could not even open my eyes. I raised my right hand to wipe away the perspiration with my sleeve and could see that Liang was carrying all kinds of equipment: a field pack, haversack, pistol, canteen, a small spade, a commander's flag, a pair of field glasses; what's more, his body was hung with two rifles, and on his shoulder rested the barrel of an 8.2 recoilless cannon. I was surprised to see that this thin, camel-like company commander could actually carry as much as a camel.

At this point, three soldiers who had fallen behind hurried up to Liang and, with sheepish looks, took back the arms that belonged to them.

All of the soldiers looked as though they had just been dragged out of a river. Liang Sanxi ordered Jin Kailai, the artillery platoon leader, to take the lead; Liang himself trailed behind them to walk with me.

"Don't worry. You'll get used to it in time," he said evenly. "Everybody has his strong points. I'll take charge of the military training, and you can concentrate on the ideological work."

He seemed to be the type that was tolerant toward others.

"All right," I said, nodding in agreement and feeling a bit touched.

Even though I wasn't carrying anything except a pistol, my legs felt like they had been filled with lead and my bones seemed to be coming apart. I wondered if I were having a hypoglycemia attack—all the energy in my blood had been drained away.

I did some detailed calculations later and found that on a full-dress, cross-country march, the gear for infantry men was still lighter than it was for the artillery troops. In the 8.2 recoilless squad, the average load for each soldier was 89 jin! Saddled like oxen with a heavy load, they still had to gallop toward the enemy like stallions.

The soldiers had been practicing light weapons firing before I arrived. According to regulations, company officers had to pass an examination by demonstrating their mastery of all the weapons used by their company. I was so worried about getting a bad record and losing face that I spent three long days lying on my belly along with the other soldiers on the practice range; it also gave me the chance to develop my interest in shooting.

Next came the examination in light-arm precision shooting for the third quarter of the year. Liang Sanxi was the first to walk onto the firing range. He won an "Excellent" mark in every category. However, nobody looked very surprised about it. This seemed to be their commander's specialty, nothing new as far as they were concerned.

I used to like to play around with pistols, although it was only a hobby. But that day my hobby saved me from disgrace. I scored a "Good" in pistol firing and passed all the other tests except light machine-gun firing.

Liang was wreathed in a smile. "Instructor, you're really great! Only three days' practice. Good. You did a good job."

Next was collective firing, squad by squad from First Platoon. Squads One and Two did a splendid job. When it was Squad Three's turn to shoot, soldier Duan Yuguo fired eight shots but only scored seventeen points.

Zhao Mengsheng stopped here and turned to Duan Yuguo. "Hey! Xiao Duan. What were you like back then? Why don't you tell it yourself?"

Duan Yuguo smiled and said, "As for myself, I really was ashamed. I joined the army in Xiamen. My father is a manager at the

International Handicrafts Trade Corporation. My mother also works in a department for foreign affairs. How could I have been prepared to endure the hard life of a soldier? I had read a few foreign novels and therefore considered myself to be the scholar of the company. I even dreamed of becoming the Chinese Victor Hugo. In particular, I looked down on the country boys who joined the army. I thought they could hardly have a single aesthetic cell in their body, and that they reeked of dried sweet potatoes from head to foot. But to them, I reeked of Western influences, and earned the nickname Aesthetic Cell.

"One day, when Instructor Wang was giving us a lecture on politics, I turned on my pocket radio and played it loud enough to be heard all over the room. Instructor Wang asked me to stand up and turn off my radio. Instead, I turned it up louder and said impudently, 'Listen! This is the Central Broadcasting Station, the great voice of the Party Central Committee—much, much more important than your program.'

"From this, you can see what I was like then. Oh well, I was only a minor character. Why don't we ask Instructor Zhao to go on with the story?"

Zhao Mengsheng gave a faint smile and continued.

At that point, Xiao Duan found himself surrounded by the soldiers of Squad Three, and by their ridicule.

"Oh, I say, Aesthetic Cell, where did you 'art off all our bullets?"

"A new soldier but an old burden. The only thing he shoots down in target practice is our squad's record."

"Hah! Are you sure he's human? His hide is even thicker than the crust of the earth."

"You'd better clean up your mouth!" Duan Yuguo shouted, wiping back the only long hair in Company Nine and looking at the others disdainfully. "It was only a few bullets that I wasted. So what? And anyway, you can't blame it on me. My rifle's no good."

Liang Sanxi came up to him and asked, "Something wrong with your rifle?"

"I said it's no good. The barrel sight is bent." Duan Yuguo looked at Liang teasingly. "Can I get another rifle and try again, like you company officers, to develop my interest in shooting?"

Liang's thick lips were vibrating. I thought he was really going to let Duan have it. Instead, he grabbed the rifle from Xiao Duan and loaded eight rounds into the magazine. He raised the rifle and took aim—standing up, too, which requires more skill than firing in the prone position.

After a whistle, the firing range became quiet.

Crack! Crack! Liang was finished firing before anyone knew it.

The soldiers stared intently ahead, waiting for the target reporter to wave his flag. They saw the reporter leap out of the shelter and gaze at the target for a moment. Then, carrying the target over his shoulder, he came running quickly toward them.

"Let . . . let Mr. Chinese Hugo . . . " he said, out of breath, "have a look for himself!"

The soldiers crowded around the target and leaped with joy. "Seventy-eight points! Seventy-eight points!"

"Hey, Aesthetic Cell, look! This is *real* art!"

"Come on. Dear Mr. Hugo, do have a look!"

Duan Yuguo was indifferent to the ridicule. He stood still, his head tilted away from the crowd. "It's no big deal . . . even if you got eighty points."

"What did you say!" Amid the roaring, the artillery platoon leader, Jin Kailai, made his way through the crowd of soldiers and pounced like a raging lion upon Duan Yuguo. Jin Kailai was a strong man, taller than average. His eyes were small under heavy brows but as sharp and bright as lightening. His body was sturdy enough to clang like armor plate. The troops called him Light Tank. He pointed at Duan with two fingers. "Duan Yuguo, what else have you got to say? Say it out to me!"

Duan lowered his eyes. He said nothing.

"Spit it out!" Jin Kailai clenched two fingers to form a fist. "It's a good thing you're not in my artillery platoon. If I were in charge of you, I wouldn't be Jin Kailai if I didn't give you a permanent case of the shits!"

Duan either gave way to the firepower of Light Tank or he finally understood the proverb, "A wise man knows how to ride the tide of his times." Duan hung his head obediently.

Three

In the burning sun and desiccating wind I crept and stumbled over the drill field. Saturday finally arrived, and that night the regiment's audiovisual team came to our company to show a movie. It was a really old one, "The Guards under Neon Lights." I didn't even feel like going to see it. Xiao Jin, the bugler, brought me a full bucket of warm water from the kitchen—I couldn't put up with any more of this until I'd had a bath.

For the six days that I had been in the company my uniform had never been dry, although I sweated less than the company commander, Liang Sanxi, and even less than the soldier Duan Yuguo. If it weren't for the fact that Xiao Jin had washed all the clothes that I threw under the bed yesterday, I wouldn't have had anything to change into.

The bath made me feel a little more relaxed. I really did intend to wash the heap of sweat-stained uniforms and underwear, but my arms ached too much to do any work. So I kicked the stuff under my bed. Maybe Xiao Jin would volunteer to help me wash them again. Why not let him learn from Lei Feng?

Of course, I knew that the political instructor ought to be a role model for leading the simple life. After I got to the company, I demoted my smoking pleasure from filter-tipped Chunghwa cigarettes to more proletarian Da Qianmens. But since it was Saturday night and no one was around, I took the opportunity to open up my small suitcase. First, I spent some time looking over my Yashika camera. Then I took out a pack of Chunghwa. I lit up, leaned back against my folded quilt, and began to enjoy the cigarette. When I closed my eyes, the multifarious life of the Small Circle flashed across my mind again.

Not too long ago—last July and August—Liu Lan started her summer vacation from studies at the Army Medical University. To make the most of that, I arranged to take my leave at the same time. We both went home to visit my parents and the city we missed so much. Our childhood friends, one after the other, came by to invite Liu Lan and me into their Small Circle.

Liu Lan and I had been considered "romantic" by our military comrades, and yet we felt ashamed of our appearance compared to those fashionable men and women in the Small Circle. Not until then did we realize that we were not at all superior, just a couple of country soldiers.

"The green uniform isn't popular anymore. It's time for you to come back."

"So you two 'old PLA' are still learning from Lei Feng. See how *we* learn," said our old chums as a friendly but ironic joke.

The Small Circle gave family dances: tango, rumba, disco, face-to-face; they compared family modernizations—little Sanyo, big Sony, Snowflake refrigerator; perfume, lipstick, and dresses as thin as the wings of a cicada made the men and women dizzy. They had seen through the mundane world; whiskey or brandy with Coca-Cola left them drunk as a sow.

Liu Lan and I were dazzled. She got her leave extended for another ten days, on the excuse that she had "caught the flu"; I returned to my post ten days late, too, my excuse being that I'd "had a high fever." My common sense told me that the people in the Small Circle lived a life of abundance and comfort but one that was devoid of any real meaning. Still, my heart was yearning: Liu Lan and I really enjoyed that style of living. And why not?

"Hey, Instructor—come on out," shouted the artillery platoon leader, Jin Kailai, as he was stepping into the room. "Let's deal those pasteboards!"

I could tell the movie was over. Out of politeness—since I was the newcomer—I picked up a fresh pack of Da Qianmens and stepped out of the back room. Liang Sanxi and the other three platoon leaders had all shown up. We sat down around the huge desk formed by four oblong tables.

Jin Kailai banged two packs of cards down on the table, then drew out one of my Da Qianmens and slapped the pack down in the middle of the desk. "Instructor's taste in cigarettes is none too poor, is it, brothers? Let's share it." As he spoke, he took an unopened pack of Sanqi cigarettes out of his pocket and put it out on the table next to mine. "We're not quitting until we've smoked up every one of them."

He seemed to be the kind of guy who was loyal to his friends. This "Light Tank" didn't look at all the way he did when he lost his temper. Now there was a lively look in his eyes.

Liang Sanxi had already lit up his hand-rolled cigarette, which was wide as a finger. He took a deep drag, exhaled, and said, "Come on. Everybody's worn out. Let's knock off for tonight."

"I knew you wouldn't be in the mood for cards after seeing that movie." Jin Kailai gave Liang a sidelong glance. "You want to get to bed early so you can meet that village girl, 'Chunni,' in your dreams, don't you?"

Liang gave a light smile, exhaling the smoke softly.

"Instructor, you may not realize it, but if they showed 'The Guards under Neon Lights' a hundred times in a row, he'd sit through it all one hundred times. Do you know why?" Jin paused, to build up the suspense. Then he went on. "Poor as our commander is, he is lucky enough to have a beautiful wife. Her name is Han Yuxiu and she looks just like that actress who plays Chunni—Tao . . . Tao *what*?"

"Tao Yuling," said the leader of Platoon One, the youngest among us.

"Right. And it's known by the whole company that Han Yuxiu is a ringer for Tao Yuling. And she is even more kind-hearted than Chunni in the movie." Jin winked at me. "Look, whenever anyone mentions Chunni, our commander will grin from ear to ear."

True enough, Liang's face was wreathed in smiles. It was the first time that I'd seen him smile so sweetly.

"But may God damn that jackass husband of Chunni's. Why, that Chen Xi should have pissed in a pot and looked at himself in the reflection. There he was—with a good wife like Chunni—and he still wanted to get divorced." Jin Kailai was getting wrapped up in his own commentary on the movie they had just seen. "If I had a beautiful and kind-hearted wife like Chunni, I would come back as an ox or a horse for her in my next life. The fact is, my wife, the big gunnysack, is great only in weight."

The Platoon One leader sniggered. "If your wife hears that . . . ."

"What do I care? She's just a contract worker in a commune cotton oil factory. Every sentence of mine is 'the highest instruction' to her." Then he grabbed the deck of cards. "So much for wives. Let's play cards. What'll it be: Trying for the Best, or Promotion?"

Seeing that Liang and I showed no interest in playing, Jin Kailai put the cards back down. He said to Liang Sanxi earnestly, "Commander, don't go on waiting around like this. You need a vacation."

Liang looked at me. "After Instructor gets familiar with the situation here, I'll go."

"If you do decide to go, you'd better leave right now. Han Yuxiu is hatching an egg." Jin Kailai looked at Liang Sanxi jokingly and counted on his fingers. "Xiao Han came to our company in March. April . . . May . . . June. Hmmm, she's having the baby in December. What's the fun of it if you wait till she has the baby?" He gave an amused smile and cursed under his breath. "Dammit. A couple lives apart, five thousand li from each other, and we only get a month's leave each year. It's either feast or famine."

The three platoon leaders rocked with laughter.

Liang Sanxi said, "Say, Platoon Leader, can't you be a little more civilized when you talk?"

"So, you don't want to play cards and you think I'm uncivilized when I talk about wives! Then how am I supposed to while away this weekend? All right, I'll talk business." Jin stood up and spoke to me in all seriousness. "Instructor, you're a newcomer and you don't know me too well. I've been thinking about having a heart-to-heart talk with you. Right here in front of everybody I'd like to tell you what's really on my mind. Next time you go to a meeting at regiment headquarters, please report to the superior that I firmly request to leave active duty when the next batch of officers is discharged to civilian work. Why? Because some of those leaders look down on me, like I was a chicken rib. A chicken rib is meatless and hard to gnaw on. It doesn't have any taste when you chew it, and yet—they're still not ready to throw it away. I don't want to play that role—to wait until I'm thrown away. All I want to do is to live with my wife and child, to eat warm soup, and have hot water whenever I want it. Oh well, I'm going to turn in and get a good night's sleep." Finishing his speech, the greatest complainer turned his back and left the room.

The conversation broke off on a sour note. Seeing that a card game was now out of the question, the other three platoon leaders left, too.

Liang said to me, "That artillery platoon leader may be pretty crude sometimes, but he's an honest person. He's been a platoon leader for almost six years. I'd say he's the most qualified platoon leader in the whole regiment. And when it comes to the 8.2 recoilless cannon and 4.0 rocket launcher, he's number one among all the artillery platoon leaders. He's also first-rate at infantry tactics. His leadership style might be kind of harsh, but he cares about his troops and he's not just talk—he performs." After a pause, he sighed. "But the man likes to complain too much. He criticizes his superiors. He's got a sharp tongue, too. I don't know how many times our company and our battalion have recommended him to be the vice-company commander, but the superiors won't hear of it."

I remained silent. Liang seemed to be depressed and sat silent for a while, too. Then he said, "We'll gradually get to know each other. It's late now. Let's turn in."

We went into the back room. He moved out a big carton and opened it, saying that he would find some clothes to change into tomorrow.

He didn't even have a wicker trunk. Everything he owned seemed to be in this carton. There were two uniforms, both very worn and one with patches on it. Other soldiers had told me that the infantry unit in charge of military training didn't have enough uniforms to wear. This company commander, of course, was no exception. There was one big plastic bag in the carton that had a new uniform overcoat in it. I asked him if this overcoat had been issued recently.

"No. It was issued last National Day."

I also wondered why he, the company commander, did not even have a watch, and why he always smoked black tobacco powder. I knew that his hometown was on Yimeng Mountain—and I myself was born there during the war. We should have had a lot to talk about. But since he didn't know that I was the son of a senior cadre—nor did he have any idea why I had come to Company Nine—there wasn't any need for me to talk about Yimeng Mountain with him.

I lay awake on my bed, unable to sleep because my whole body ached with pain. I heard Liang also turn over in bed from time to time.

After a long while he must have thought that I had fallen asleep, and he struck a match to light up his cigarette. A guy like him could take any hardship. Maybe he was lonely, too. I supposed he must be thinking about his "Chunni."

I don't know when I dozed off. The splashing of rainfall outside woke me up. Half awake, I heard Liang get out of bed. The sound of him fastening his belt told me that he was going to make the night rounds of soldiers' beds and guard posts.

As he tiptoed out of the room a sense of pity welled up in my heart. Commanders like him, as well as those simple-minded soldiers, no doubt were all devoted to their duty. But while I might sympathize with them, pity them, or even praise them, I could not imagine working and living with them for very long.

Damn! This so-called "smelting furnace" company—this *real* career soldier! How could I endure the life in this place without the disciplines of a monk? I cursed "Thunder God" again. If I hadn't needed to keep away from him, I would never have had to play the "curvilinear transfer" game and come here.

Four

Individual Demolition
Earthworks Construction
Offensive Formations Practice
Dual Bayonet Assault
Weekend Drill Practice

Each was checked off the list one after the other by regimental headquarters according to the drill regulations schedule. The company political instructor had to be tested without exception, just like any fighter. A political instructor's work covered all kinds of areas: the personnel component of the Party branch at the post, the quarterly reviews, evaluations of each soldier's work, inductions of new members into the Party, heart-to-heart talks. The regimental political department was demanding that I insert ideological work into the drill field. I found myself unable to bear up.

The thing I dreaded most was the full-dress, ten-kilometer cross-country march every Tuesday morning. Although I never once made it to the end, I still always ended up with cramps in my calves, and once almost collapsed.

What's worse, the three meals a day, which provided us with calories, made life even more difficult for me. Even if we did have plenty of steamed bread, rice, and corn flour to fill us up, the stuff that came along with it was awful. I wondered how Liang Sanxi and the soldiers could eat it with such enjoyment, even if the Creator did issue us all the same digestive system. Time and again I asked the chief cook to improve the food, but he'd just complain: "The allocation for provisions stays the same while the prices go up every day." The only improvement he could make was to cook some "gold and silver rolls"—made from corn and wheat flour—or to fold the food in flour wrappers. Since my company was stationed in a remote mountain area, there was no restaurant to go to even if I'd had the money. Once, I bought some refreshments during a meeting at the regiment headquarters. I was so afraid I'd be seen that I could only wolf down one or two pieces when I was alone for a moment, sneaking like a thief.

I counted the days on my fingers; it was still two days shy of one full month since I had arrived. I looked in the mirror: the face was much darker; I touched my cheek—it was much thinner. Each time I took a bath it seemed that my body was melting away, one layer after another.

I had written two letters to my mother, urging her to take the "diplomatic offensive" as soon as possible. Mother replied that she had made plans to settle me in the Office of Information in her military region, where I would work as a cameraman—that was no problem. However, she had met with difficulties in transferring me out. She had written to the leader of my division and talked with him on the telephone long distance. The answer was that he could not act too hastily. The situation was no longer what it had been a few years ago. Hasty action might be too obvious and cause problems. He suggested that I stay in the company for another half year before I transfer again.

My God! Another half year? I would turn into a "thin camel," too.

One day, I went to battalion headquarters for a meeting and got back after lunchtime. I mindlessly ate some of the food the kitchen police had reserved for me in the dining room and then went back to the headquarters. Resting my back against the folded quilt, I was soon lost in thought.

The call to emergency muster sounded suddenly. I hurriedly buckled my belt and got out of the room.

I saw the whole company lining up in front of the dining room. Liang Sanxi, livid with anger, was facing his soldiers and speaking to them. " . . . shocking! Such behavior is really shocking!"

I never thought he could be so fierce when he lost his temper. I could only wonder what shocking event had happened in the company, so I stepped into line quietly and tried to take it all in.

"Steamed bread:—someone threw a loaf of snow-white steamed bread into the pigswill vat!" Liang slapped himself on the chest. "Comrades, let's search our hearts. Do we still have feelings? The feelings of the working class? Well! Yes or no?"

I was stupefied. During my lunch just now, I had eaten only half of the steamed bread that the cooking squad left for me and then I threw the rest of it into the pigswill vat.

"Dismiss!" Liang roared, with a wave of his hand. "Go there and have a look for yourselves!"

The soldiers crowded around the pigswill vat near the dining room, whispering to each other.

Jin Kailai confronted Duan. "Duan Yuguo, you playboy—were you the one that did it?"

Duan glared at him. "You always bully the weak. I swear by God: whoever did it is a bastard!"

Not until the leader of Squad Three came forward to verify that he had not seen Duan throw the steamed bread away during lunchtime did Jin Kailai quiet down. Liang was still angry.

"Whoever threw it can tell his squad leader or platoon leader individually. Each squad is going to hold a meeting tonight to discuss this playboy's life style."

I was, perhaps, too sensitive about the word "playboy." I felt sure that Liang was seizing upon the "bread event" to single me out as the target of his attack and to embarrass me in his roundabout way. Fuming inside, I rushed into the headquarters and lay down on my bed. A while later, Liang came in. I said to him in a huff, "Comrade Commander, there are more direct ways to make me the target of your attack. Don't use those Cultural Revolution tactics—stir up the masses first. I'm the one who threw the bread away!"

"Instructor, I . . . I didn't know that you'd come back from battalion headquarters. Honest, I really didn't think that you threw the bread away. If I had, I would have talked with you individually," explained Liang, quite embarrassed.

I rudely turned my back to him and faced the wall. I heard him sigh.

"Instructor, don't ever let this affect our unity. I'm not trying to explain myself, but I . . . I've never been one for getting at people behind their back. I worked together with Instructor Wang for three years. We used to argue or quarrel or sometimes even get a little red in the face, but we always stayed united, really as close to each other as brothers."

I said nothing. After a pause, he stammered: "I'll ask the bugler, Xiao Jin, to notify each squad that the meeting tonight is . . . is called off."

I did not talk to Liang for three days.

Later, one afternoon when Liang Sanxi was away, Duan Yuguo of Squad Three slipped into the headquarters.

"Instructor, don't bother to get angry with Seven Tufts," he said, studying my face at the same time. "The month before last, I threw a piece of steamed bread into the pigswill vat and got lectured by Seven Tufts, too."

"Who's Seven Tufts?"

"Ah, that's the nickname I gave Commander, drawing upon my artistic creativity." Duan laughed triumphantly. He picked up the toothbrush out of Liang's old military brushing mug. "Look, Instructor, the toothbrush he uses looks as if it had just been picked up out of a garbage heap. One, two, three . . . oh, wait; not seven, it's *nine* tufts. No! Look—another tuft is falling out. So, let's call him Eight Tufts."

I didn't answer. Even though I had never counted the tufts on Liang's toothbrush, I knew from rooming with him for a month that he was a hick who wouldn't waste a single penny.

"An officer—earning 60 yuan a month—and he won't even buy a new toothbrush." Duan tossed Eight Tufts' toothbrush back into the mug. "Save money—that's the only thing he understands: saving money. Typical peasant ideology! The whole world is going after consumer goods. They say the Japanese never wash clothes. They just throw dirty clothes into the trash and change into new ones. Meanwhile here, Eight Tufts is still criticizing us for throwing away some bread. That's really the most ridiculous thing in the world."

I realized that Duan had come in here looking for an ally, as if he could set up a "united front" with me. As disdainful as I was about Liang Sanxi, I, a political instructor, would never even consider mixing with an ordinary soldier like Duan.

Plainly seeing that I did not feel like talking, Duan persisted in trying to strike up a conversation. "Instructor, why don't you get moving and get yourself transferred out of here?"

I jumped. "Who told you I'm going to get transferred?"

He laughed. "I don't need to be told. I figured it out myself."

I straightened my face. "Why, you . . . . "

"Nothing to be afraid of," he said. He paused for a moment, then asked, "Instructor, they say your father is a high-ranking officer. Is he sixth rank or seventh?"

"Rubbish!" I flared up in anger.

"So, ho! I do know something about you." He was still grinning. "Isn't it clear as daylight that you and I can never have anything in common with bumpkins like Eight Tufts? I'm going to put in for a discharge at the end of the year." Then he tried to ingratiate himself to me. "Instructor, if you want to buy big color TVs, tape recorders, any of that kind of stuff, just tell me. Both of my parents work in foreign affairs departments. It's as easy as one, two, three for me, Duan Yuguo, to buy import goods. As for the price, I can guarantee you half of the market price."

"I will not ask you to buy anything for me. Back off."

Finally facing up to my coolness, Duan went out looking displeased.

Liang Sanxi's application for leave went through in the middle of October. Several times he had packed his baggage and then as many times unpacked it.

I could tell that his thoughts were complex and contradictory. He wanted to go, but he felt he could not. He had obviously understood that I was by no means qualified to be an instructor. He was afraid that I would make a mess of the company while he was away.

Soon afterward, Liang spent a whole day in meetings about military training at the regimental headquarters, and didn't get back until after 8:00 P.M. Under the hanging light, he told me the gist of the meeting, that the year-end test was coming up and that we should put more effort into our work. Then he stared at me. "Instructor, I decided to go on leave tomorrow, so I wouldn't miss the year-end test. What do you think about it?"

"Do whatever you want to," I answered casually.

He rolled a cigarette with his black tobacco powder, took two drags, and said to me uneasily, "Instructor, I'm a man who can't hold back what's on his mind. I had heard it before, and I heard it again today at the meeting at regimental headquarters . . . the rumor about your transfer."

I was startled.

He went on. "I'm sure it is just that—a rumor. But if you are leaving, I'll put off my vacation; if not, I'm leaving tomorrow."

Now that it was out in the open, I didn't have anything to lose. I said to him in an angry voice, "Go take your leave or don't take it. Make up your own mind. As for the talk about me, each man has his own tongue and I don't try to stop anyone from saying whatever he wants to. But I have not been informed that I'm getting a transfer yet."

He said nothing. The next day he did not set off. After that, he never mentioned his vacation again.

My falling-out with Liang and the other company officers became more and more obvious. The company headquarters were empty on Saturday evenings—nobody came to play cards anymore, to talk about wives, or make jokes around me.

One day I gave the company a lecture on "General Inculcation of War Preparedness." The regimental political department had planned for me to talk to the soldiers about the Vietnamese armed provocations along the border in recent years. The idea was to build up the soldiers' enthusiasm for military training. I got together some newspapers and read the soldiers several news reports about it, in addition to our Foreign Ministry's diplomatic note to the Vietnamese government. I was only repeating what the papers said, and didn't inject any personal feelings.

After the lecture, Jin Kailai came up to me and said, "Instructor, that was a wonderful lecture! Yes, that was finer than the hairs on a hen's tooth! And don't you worry: when it comes time to fight, we promise to follow your lead right into the thick of it."

All I could do was to turn my back on such sarcasm and leave quickly.

Mother was growing more and more anxious about my transfer. Every few days I would get another letter from her. She reported every step of the progress of my transfer, bemoaning the fact that she had never dealt with such a knotty affair.

I had believed that word of my "curvilinear transfer" could be kept from the soldiers. But, as we say, no wall in the world is windproof. Of course, while nobody in the outfit knew every detail of the story, all the officers had deduced that I had come to Company Nine in order to get transferred to a better situation. Even some well-informed soldiers had an idea about what was going on. They would wink at each other when I passed by.

I endured each successive day of hardship until one day at the end of November, when I received another letter from Mother. In it, she told me that my transfer was almost settled at last. She asked that I leave the company just as soon as the transfer order arrived. At the end of the letter she informed me rather cryptically that she had heard that the troops in my outfit might be going into action. She warned me, "Never spread this around! Never let anyone know!" The double *nevers* with the exclamation marks made me wonder what action our troops might be going into. It was true that the situation in the south had been tense enough. But that was only on a small scale. The firing was still far from here. I ignored Mother's warning. When I was alone, I called up the leader of my division, who had been helping me with my transfer, and inquired in a roundabout way as to the possibility of our seeing action. He burst into laughter, saying that he had heard nothing so far, and that my mother was too neurotic.

It calmed my fears. Still, I could hardly bear staying in the company for even one more day.

One Saturday evening, when I was coming back to the barracks from a stroll by the mountain stream, I heard Liang Sanxi and Jin Kailai talking loudly from the headquarters window. I stopped to listen quietly.

Jin Kailai was saying, "Commander, you don't have anything new except that dress overcoat. What are you messing around with this stuff for?"

"You'd better pack up your things, Kailai. We're moving out," said Liang.

"Moving out? Where in the hell are we moving out to?"

"Down south. Don't you think there's going to be a fight?"

"Yes," said Jin Kailai, "it does seem like there's a battle brewing. But there are so many troops all over the country. How do you know we're the ones that are going to the front?"

"No more questions. Let's wait and see."

Jin Kailai persisted. "Commander, isn't it the superiors who tipped you off? Come on, are you going to keep it a secret from me?"

"No superior ever gave me a hint. What only the company commander should know is known by practically everybody."

"Then you . . . ."

"I got the information from Instructor's mother," said Liang Sanxi.

"That's too much! How could that old biddy give you any information?"

"You really are straightforward," said Liang. "Don't you wonder why she has been so anxious about Instructor's transfer? Recently, I heard from the clerk in charge of regimental personnel that Instructor's mother phones the division headquarters almost every day."

"Hmm, that could be," said Jin Kailai. "I heard the old bat is really skillful. She can be more well-informed than a division commander—or a corps commander."

"That's about it. I figure our troops will move out to the front in eight or ten days. You've got to keep it a secret," Liang said. "Never breathe a word about it."

"Damn it," said Jin Kailai. "If that old bag dares to get her son transferred out right when the troops are going to the front, just watch me go to Beijing and sue her at my own expense."

My transfer order came through ten days later.

It turned out that Liang Sanxi was a real prophet. When I was just about to leave, an order arrived for our troops to start for the front. The same day, the kitchen police butchered four pigs, but there was no time for tasting them.

I found it difficult to move forward, but more difficult to move backward. I was in a dilemma.

"Get out of here! Go on and get out of here right now!" The tolerant Liang Sanxi suddenly turned into a Jin Kailai. He fired a volley of curses at me. "Damn you! Yes, you can get away with your damned sealed order! I can ask the superiors to send a new political instructor. But, 'Maintain an army for a thousand days to use it for an hour.' Soldier, you ought to know what being a soldier means! This is your moment of truth. You can take a step either forward or backward. If you choose backward, what will you be? There are plenty of words to describe that! You had better go think about it!"

Five

The troop train of modified boxcars carrying weapons and soldiers snaked along day and night. Company Nine occupied two cars and there I sat in one of them, the political instructor who dared not retreat, even though I held the transfer order in my hand.

I understood well enough—even without Liang Sanxi's unrestrained curses—that a PLA soldier is to be ready to sacrifice his life on the battlefield without a moment's hesitation. If I had walked out on the troops then, I would have stained the honor of our military; a deserter and a traitor are exactly what I would have been.

When we finally arrived at the "border defense," we realized that this stretch of the border actually had no defense at all. We could see with our naked eyes the permanent as well as temporary enemy fortifications one after the other on the far bank of the Red River. With our telescopes, we had no trouble seeing the pitch-black muzzles of rifles aimed at our chests. Never mind that for years we Chinese had been shouting that our country was Vietnam's own vast retreating area.

Since we had no choice but to fight, everything now seemed urgent, and was hurriedly done. With so many troops arriving all at once, striking a camp became the top priority. The headquarters for all officers above regimental level was crammed together into the local administration offices unit. The company camps were spread out over the mountains and built with green bamboo, thatched grass, palm leaves, and tarpaulin covers. As a defense against air attack or cannon fire, the soldiers often had to stay inside the damp, freshly dug "cat ear holes," which had been developed for use in this particular border situation.

We listened to the cries of outrage from the people who used to live in this region but who had been left homeless by the attacks. We witnessed the miserable sight of the Hekou County Nursery after it was strafed by Vietnamese machine gun fire. Written requests for active duty poured into the company headquarters. A few soldiers bit open their middle fingers and wrote down their vows against the enemy in blood, although it had not been encouraged by the superiors. But, as the political instructor who traveled to this place with Company Nine, I was still feeling alienated and uncomfortable. How I regretted ever giving up the cushy job I had held at the corps' institute just to come to Company Nine for a curvilinear transfer! Self does, self has, they say. My only hope, even then, was to leave this combat-ready outfit and get back to the institute.

I secretly visited my close friends at the corps' institute and asked them to help me transfer back, under the pretext that the work required me to be there. But just at that moment, a stern order came from the corps' Party Committee that no high-ranking cadre's son or daughter now serving in a military unit could transfer out to the corps' institute. Any and all who had recently transferred out would have to return to their units at once. The few people who really were needed by the institute during wartime—officers and soldiers alike—would have to have their transfers approved by the corps' Party Committee. Anyone who disobeyed would be disciplined according to martial law.

The news disheartened me.

Liang Sanxi was, I should say, friendly with me. When he stood there cursing me as I was about to leave the company, I had said nothing back to him. Now, seeing that I was still present, he dropped his scornful attitude towards me. Instead, he often consulted with me on the activities of the company as he did when I had first arrived. I also noticed that he had persuaded the other officers to be kinder to me. On the way to the front, for example, Jin Kailai kept making sarcastic remarks to me. He said he was going to keep an eye on me out on the battlefield and if I even looked like I was going to turn around, he said he'd give me a taste of his bullets. But now, although he still was not very friendly, he at least had quit being belligerent.

Accelerated prewar training began for the company. The regimental officers demanded that we all learn to adapt to the hilly terrain by climbing mountains and crawling through the jungle. That was even more dreadful than those full-dress, ten-kilometer cross-country marches. Liang Sanxi was so worn out that his voice became hoarse, his eyeballs red and swollen, his lips chapped, and his thin face still thinner. Even Jin Kailai, despite the nickname "Light Tank," developed sunken cheeks. To say nothing of me. I was too exhausted to take my clothes off before falling asleep at night. It often occurred to me that I'd rather be hit by a stray bullet than to endure these hardships.

I had been out of touch with Mother for over twenty days. Now that I was at the front, I expected her to be at her wits' end, but I was in no mood to write to her. Then, a batch of letters was forwarded to the company from the rear office. I received three. One was from Liu Lan at the Army Medical University. She asked in the letter why I did not come back after receiving the transfer order, and scornfully accused me of trying to be a hero. She wrote, without trying to conceal it, that the college students nowadays admire the bronze monument on Liberty Island in New York and do not care about Spartacus. The other two letters were written by Mother. In the first, she told me to send her a telegram before I left the company so she could have a car waiting at the station to meet me. But the situation had taken on a turn for the worse by the time she wrote the second letter. She seemed to have realized the difficulties involved in getting me transferred. She asked if gossip about me had kept me from leaving. She concluded that it would be better for me to leave the company and get back to the corps' institute if it really had become impossible to transfer out of the outfit completely.

That was exactly the decision I had come to.

How I hoped to leave Company Nine and get back to the corps headquarters now! However, my only hope lay in the hands of Corps Commander Lei, "Thunder God." I recalled the story Mother had told me many times about how she had saved Thunder God's life.

It was in the fall of 1943. About 30,000 Japanese invaders, together with puppet government troops, began a large-scale mopping up operation in the Yimeng Mountain area. Corps Commander Lei was then the commander of Battalion One, the Independent Regiment of the Shandong Military Region. My mother was political instructor at the underground hospital attached to the Independent Regiment. Battalion One was besieged by the enemy while covering the retreat of the Party's Institute of Shandong and Bohai Bank. Commander

Lei—Thunder God—headed the whole battalion into the bloody battle. The battle went on from ten o'clock in the morning to dusk, until the institutes had safely retreated. But of the more than 400 fighters under Thunder God's command, fewer than 100 were left, and most of them were wounded. Thunder God, himself seriously wounded, was left lying in a pool of blood to breathe his last. Mother was then doing rescue work on the battlefield. Hidden by night, braving the storm of bullets and shells, she searched through the heaps of corpses for any wounded who were still alive. When she felt Thunder God's mouth and found him to be still breathing, she lifted him onto her shoulder and crept back over the bodies of the dead.

Mother settled Thunder God into a concealed cave to hide him from the enemy's search-and-destroy mop-up. She cut off her pitch-black hair, put on an old felt cap that she borrowed from a villager, and tied her waist with a coarse rope; disguised as a poor boy watching over the forest lands, she looked after Thunder God day and night. Mother searched near and far to find medicine for him. She boiled her only bed sheet and tore it into strips for bandages.

One night, during a thunderstorm, Mother heard strange noises coming from outside the cave. She stepped out and, during a flash of lightening, saw four or five wolves rushing toward the mouth of the cave, peering through green eyes and howling. Obviously, they had detected the putrid scent of Thunder God's wounds. Mother held a loaded Mauser, but she was afraid of giving away her position and she dared not fire. So she seized a pickaxe and faced down the wolves at the front of the cave until daybreak.

Mother endured all the hardships a woman could ever bear and took good care of Thunder God, who finally did recover.

On the day that Thunder God set out to return to his troops, he held Mother's hand tightly and said, "An honorable man would do anything to pay back a dept of gratitude. Wherever I go, I will never forget that you are a true heroine."

That was really a friendship of life and death! Would he, Thunder God, be alive today and be the corps commander if it had not been for my mother? Although he might cultivate his image as a modern-day version of the ancient, incorruptible Judge Bao, Mother's request nevertheless would come to him in a moment of crisis. Could he really refuse to help me, the only son of his rescuer? What's more, I used to work in the corps' institute, and the institute was joining the war effort. He wouldn't be overstepping the bounds of propriety to transfer me back there. One sentence from Thunder God—"It's for the sake of the work at the institute"—and my return there would be completely justified.

Thinking along these lines, I wrote a letter to Mother and hurriedly mailed it.

We spent Spring Festival at the front. After that, the officers in each company again returned to action alert. The vice-commander of Company Nine was transferred to the reconnaissance unit at regimental headquarters as a staff officer; Jin Kailai, who had complained that he was a chicken rib, was now appointed company vice-commander.

Another unbearable week passed. I reckoned that Mother had received my letter. How I hoped she would write to Thunder God as soon as possible!

The prewar training ended. Now each company was checking and rechecking its equipment, the soldiers trying to regain their lost strength.

But too late! It was too late to carry out my planned transfer: On the night of February 14, the division headquarters called together all officers from platoon leader and up to see the restricted movie *Patton*. It was 11:00 P.M. when the movie ended; still, the division's chief of staff announced over the microphone in a loud voice that the corps commander had been carefully examining the battle plan for our division and would soon be arriving to make a speech. He asked us to wait quietly for a moment.

"Oh, *our* Patton is going to speak to us!" someone said in a low voice.

I knew that after they saw the movie they would naturally associate our corps commander with General Patton.

A moment later soldiers in the crowd were stretching their necks and whispering that the corps commander was coming. I looked up. Yes. It was Thunder God.

Commander Lei was no taller than 1.7 meters. He was a thin but agile old man who never did have the stature of General Patton. Yet, for his colleagues, he was more awe-inspiring than Patton. He always walked in a stride of 75 centimeters at each step, according to drill regulations, with his back rigid and his eyes looking forward. His every movement was filled with the bearing of a military man and the dignity of a general.

The corps commander looked around the open air meeting place. His confident manner seemed a reflection of his own and his corps' invincibility. Then Thunder God took off his cap and slammed it on the table. The microphone jumped. The meeting place suddenly got quiet, so quiet that a leaf could fall and be heard quite clearly. In our corps, everyone knew the stories about Corps Commander Lei banging down his cap.

In 1967, the leftists had decided to take control of the municipal Party committee in the city of C., where the corps institute was stationed. Kang Sheng, advisor to the Central Group of the Cultural Revolution, telephoned the corps and ordered the troops there to support the leftists' seizure of power. Kang had said that a cadre from the corps could preside over the new Red political structure. However, a pro-left group from the corps had already reported back to the commander, informing Lei that the leader of the leftists was actually a pilferer; the cadre who stood ready to take over as head of the new Red political force was a slippery fellow that Commander Lei had disliked very much.

The commander called a meeting of the corps' Party committee. He slammed his cap angrily on the table and said, "Anyone willing to risk dismissal can stay in this meeting. But this is one person who will never collaborate with that rabble trying to take over the municipal Party committee. Anyone afraid of dismissal from office can get out of here and go take a high post in the new Red Power."

Lei's slamming of his cap got him removed from office and taken into custody. When, after a year, the leftists' behavior had become so outrageous that they lost the favor of the Central Group of the Cultural Revolution, Lei was able to return as commander of the corps. The conference records of the corps Party committee showed that in ten years the commander had thrown down his cap four times—each bringing him bad luck.

Now, why was Thunder God throwing down his cap again? We were all dumbfounded.

Lei paced up and down the rostrum, finally standing still—arms akimbo—and appearing to be in a towering rage. A thundering shout came through the microphone: "A curse on you! Somebody here tonight is going to get it!" Nobody could guess why the commander was so angry, or who was in for it.

"Damn it!" roared Lei. "Don't you know? My cannon are set to roar; my armored cars are ready to rumble onward; my soldiers are going out to kill the enemy! Our soldiers will bleed—and many will sacrifice their lives! But just now . . . there was a resourceful lady. . . so resourceful that she could call me from hundreds of miles behind my forward post! Right now, every minute of time on my telephone is priceless. And why did that lady call me up? She wanted me to take special care of her son— through backdoor connections! *Damnation!* *Lady*? Hah! A whore! She is as brazen as she is shameless. And what is her son? Well, he used to work in our corps' institute but now he's a political instructor in some company in your division! . . . "

I was in a daze. I felt as if my head had exploded. The commander was cursing my mother and me without mentioning our names. He continued: "Damn it! She was so bold as to try a backdoor deal on this battlefield! I set her straight! I wouldn't care if she was Mrs. Heaven or Madame God. Anyone who would dare to make a backdoor deal on *this* battlefield—her son is going to carry the explosives right up to the enemy's blockhouse! *He* will do it!"

The storm of applause lasted for over a minute, drowning out a portion of Thunder God's curse. I didn't hear anything of what the commander was saying next. I could tell that the applause was growing more and more intense, heaping the ridicule upon me, whipping me with shame.

I was nearly out of my head. I don't know how Liang Sanxi or any of the others kept me on the troop truck or how I got into the company tent. When I finally came to, I wept uncontrollably.

"What's the use of your damned crying?" Liang Sanxi said angrily. "Too far. Your mother went too far. She was shameless in the way she tried to work a backdoor deal."

I kept on crying. Liang Sanxi tried to console me. "Anyone can make a mistake. So what?—as long as you can see that what you did was wrong. This fight here hasn't started yet. You will have a lot of chances on the battlefield to correct your mistakes."

My eyes dried. I fell into a daze again. At daybreak, I heard some talking inside the tent. "I swear, that biddy deserved Thunder God's curse!" "Before anyone tries to desert, I'll shoot him dead first!"

I couldn't identify the voices in the general clamor.

"Damn it! I don't care what you say, us country boys are the only ones they can count on in the fight." That was Jin Kailai talking loudly. "Gentlemen, when the time comes, I, the country hick, will be right out front, and you just follow me in the charge. What's the use of being afraid to die? I'll be right up front in it!"

"Hah! We've got a traitor in our company, and now we've all been disgraced." That tinny adolescent voice was Jin Xiaozhu's, the bugler who was not quite seventeen. He had worshipped me, the political instructor, ever since I came to the company, as if I were a god. But from the day I got my transfer order, Jin had wrinkled his lips and showed me the whites of his eyes.

"None of you will ever look down upon me—Duan Yuguo. I pledge my loyalty to our motherland. I'm ready to shed my blood. I will never be a deserter!"

Even Aesthetic Cell was getting courageous. I felt my numbed consciousness begin to revive and my blood to boil. A galling shame, a crowning humiliation had struck my heart like some venomous snake.

I am a man! I am mankind! I know what honor is. I was born on the fiery Yimeng battlefield. I come from a house of warriors. I will defend the dignity of mankind. I must defend the dignity of the descendant of a general!

I sat up, got out of bed. I picked up a piece of snow-white paper and rushed from the tent. A moment later I was confronting Xiao Jin with an order: "Sound the call to emergency muster for me!"

Xiao Jin was too confounded to take action.

"Call an emergency muster for me!"

Liang Sanxi came up to Xiao Jin and said in a low voice: "Sound the bugle."

Squarely facing the one hundred soldiers of Company Nine, I wailed: "From now on, anyone who says I'm afraid of death—I'll bayonet him into blood and gore! Whether I'm a hero or a coward, you'll see on the battlefield!"

Saying those words, I bit open the flesh of my middle finger, and

with my own blood I scrawled on the snow-white paper three
exclamation marks.

At this point, Zhao Mengsheng covered his face with his hands
and leaned to his knees, his shoulders shaking. I could see that he was
agonizing in self-condemnation.

A dull *clack* indicated that another cassette had been filled. After
a moment of silence, I quietly replaced the full tape with a blank one.

A good while later, Zhao raised his head. In a milder tone, he
went on with his story.

Six

Our regiment's combat mission was to stage a deep thrust attack. That meant that after the battle started, and the division launched its frontal attack, our regiment would thrust deep into the enemy position through gaps in its defense line, that way cutting off the enemy's retreat. Besides guaranteeing large numbers of troops to wipe out the enemy on the first defense line, we could secure strong points for our follow-up units in their attack on the second line. Our Third Battalion was designated the advance battalion. Company Nine would be the point company. This placed Company Nine in the most important place in the whole regiment and, indeed, the whole division—the edge of the knife, the point of the dagger!

Company Nine's most critical task was to thrust rapidly into the enemy's forward position on Height 364 at 6:00 P.M. on the day of the battle. And we would have to keep Height 364 and defend it to the last.

Height 364, as indicated on the map, was actually two hills—the highest peak and an unnamed hill—and stood more than 40 li inside the border. The strategic importance was that the hill overlooked a highway that led to the city of A. in Vietnam. The hill stood just to the left of the highway and could be used by the enemy to stall our southward advance to the city of A. Intelligence reports showed the enemy's position there to be garrisoned by a reinforced company. There were bamboo daggers, concertina wire entanglements, and mines in front of the position, and terraced entrenchments, block-houses, and an artillery position at the top of the hill.

Either because the corps commander wanted to keep his word about ordering me to be the first to charge the enemy's blockhouses, or because Company Nine had proven itself to be ahead of the whole regiment in military training, this arduous assignment was given to us. All the companies of our battalion had vied with each other for the honor of being the advance company. The battalion and regimental command both chose Company Nine and they said that the corps commander had approved their selection. But I wasn't going to bother to figure it all out. The whole company was proud of being the point company, and one thing anyone could see was that we were facing an unimaginably fierce battle.

As was customary for infantrymen going into battle, everyone in the company had his head shaved. This made it impossible for a soldier to be seized by the hair during hand-to-hand combat; it also made it easier to treat any head wounds.

The kitchen police were doing their best to improve the food. They announced that our last meal inside the country would be *jiaozi* dumplings with peeled shrimp, pork, and chives stuffing. I noticed that soldiers who only received an allowance of six yuan a month had begun to smoke filter-tipped cigarettes. Even Liang Sanxi, who always smoked low-grade tobacco powder, bought two packs of Hongtashan. Jin Kailai, who was now noticeably kinder toward me, bought two bottles of Wuliangye from who knows where, and insisted that I and other company officers share it with him.

There was nothing unusual about any of this. It simply told me that they had realized they were facing a life-and-death battle. Blood would be shed. Before they said goodbye to this world, they wanted to savor whatever sweetness life could afford them.

The company had decided that Platoon One would be the advance unit. The Party liaison held another meeting to discuss the selection of an officer to lead the platoon. Comrade Gao, the secretary in charge of news reports for the regiment, attended the meeting. As soon as we were named the advance company, he came by to collect the soldiers' written requests for battle assignment, most of which included testimonials of courage and allegiance. It was obvious that as soon as Company Nine achieved its objectives, it would be the focus of his news report.

No sooner had the members of the branch committee taken their seats than Jin Kailai got up and said: "I don't see any use for this meeting. If you looked up the records in our military history, you'd see it's an unwritten rule that the vice-company commander leads the point platoon. Since my superior has favored me with the title of vice-company commander—the officer who can expect to die first in battle—I'll validate their faith in me. You can rest assured: I'll die a terrific death as vice-company commander!"

Secretary Gao wrote nothing in his notebook. There was obviously nothing glorious in complaining.

Feeling remorseful, I said, "Let's obey the corps commander's order that I be the first one to raid the blockhouses. I'll lead the point platoon."

"Instructor, you . . . " Liang Sanxi looked at me earnestly. "Why bring that up again? Anyway, you have your own work as instructor. How could you be the person to lead the point platoon?"

Jin Kailai added, "Instructor, I've seen that you are a man with guts. I'm not going to bring up the past—and I'm not going to let you bring it up, either! From now on, we're in this together and we go through thick and thin together. The instructor is the nerve center of a company—it's just not your turn to die!"

There was no doubt about his sincerity. I was on the verge of tears.

Next, when Liang Sanxi volunteered himself to lead the point platoon, Jin Kailai stopped him sternly, too. "None of that stuff, Commander! Compared to me, Jin Kailai, you're absolutely unqualified to lead the point platoon."

Secretary Gao and I were both taken aback.

Jin Kailai continued. "As for your ability to command, I admire you, of course. And as for your military achievements, you've gone farther than I have. But here are my qualifications: I, Jin Kailai, have three brothers. Even if I do die, my old parents will still have three sons to provide for them. The ancestral graveyard won't go to pot for lack of offspring. But look at you. Your eldest brother died for the revolution, early on; your next eldest brother died for others, and miserably at that. That's why you shouldn't die, if it's not absolutely necessary." He turned to Secretary Gao and me. "You don't know about his family. And anyway, I'm not the kind of man who minces words, even if some people don't want to hear about it."

I was downhearted. I had come to the company such a long time ago and I still knew nothing of the commander's life. It appeared that his family had suffered misfortunes. But now there was no time to talk about it.

Jin Kailai wiped his wet eyes. "To tell the truth, Commander, I'm not going to care too much to see anyone in our company be 'glorious.' They just fight and lay down their lives for the country, that's all. But you, if . . . . How will your white-haired mother and Han Yuxiu live? Xiao Han must have had the baby by now, and you don't even know if it's a boy or a girl."

Liang Sanxi shook his hand. His voice was trembling. "Vice-Commander, I'm telling you . . . . I don't want you to bring it up again, ever."

My eyes were moist with tears. It was my fault. Because of my irresponsibility as instructor, he had to give up his furlough.

"All right, enough. We don't have time for a marathon meeting. Let's follow common sense—I'll lead the point platoon." Jin Kailai pretended to pick up a gavel and rap the table. From there, we went on to anticipate the problems we were going to face and talk over possible solutions. When the meeting was over, Jin Kailai grinned to Secretary Gao. "Hey, writer! If I become glorious, don't forget to sing my praises in the newspaper." He tapped his left breast pocket. "Look, there's a little notebook in here, and it's full of words of bravery. Every single sentence and word is glorious. I'm just afraid, man, that I'll step on a mine and get my notebook blown to bits, then . . . . "

Liang Sanxi said, "Vice-Commander! You . . . . "

"I'm only joking. Secretary Gao is no stranger around here. So stop worrying," said Jin Kailai.

Everything was ready, yet everything was in haste.

On the afternoon of February 16, a large detachment of seasoned troops was assigned to our regiment from both Jinan and Beijing Command. Because of our being named point company, fifteen of them were assigned to us. Apparently, they had been rushed to the front all the way from various units. The sad part is that we didn't have time to organize a welcoming meeting. We didn't even have time to register their names. They were split off two or three to each squad in time to have *jiaozi*.

The curtain of night fell. Our whole company was hidden along the bank of the Red River, awaiting orders.

During the time before the battle, the hands of the clock ruled our thoughts: the more impatient we became of their slow pace, the less inclined were the hands to hasten their leisurely steps. When the hour, minute, and second hands converged upon twelve, the night became the morning of the 17th. A cannon suddenly boomed, then came the roar of hundreds of cannon. The earth shook and the air vibrated as though in an earthquake of eight on the Richter scale! The red, whistling shells flew like shooting stars. Raging flames rose in the distance. The entire night sky glowed crimson. Under this spectacular curtain of night, countless assault craft shuttled back and forth across the Red River, ferrying thousands of soldiers to the opposite bank.

A feeling began to rise up in my mind: the Chinese nation was inviolable, but I had violated the trust bestowed upon all its descendants!

My whole company met the dawn with anxious waiting. At 7:30, the assault craft ferried us across the Red River. As soon as we got to the other bank, we saw dead and wounded soldiers being carried back from the forward position. Some emotional soldiers began to shed tears.

Jin Kailai brandished a broadsword of the type used by the Dai people in Yunnan—who knows where he found it! He swung it high over his head, the polished edge glittering in the air. "What's the use of your damned crying? Give the crying to those bastards who've been gorging themselves on our Chinese rice! Just watch me make them scream like ghosts!" Then he turned to a repatriated Chinese who had been guiding Company Nine. "Brother, you get behind me and point out the way. Platoon One, follow me!"

The point platoon penetrated the narrow valley. Liang Sanxi and I followed, leading the rest of the troops.

Before we had advanced very far we encountered Vietnamese who had been routed by our forward troops. They fired at us with antiaircraft machine guns, grenades, and submachine guns from three directions.

"Down!" Liang Sanxi quickly pushed me to the ground and then ordered, "Platoon Three, take your firing positions. Fire!"

Liang's submachine gun erupted. A moment later, Platoon Three's light and heavy machine guns roared in concert. I had no sooner taken aim at the enemy than Liang Sanxi shouted at me, "I'll stay here with Platoon Three to cover you. You lead the others to wipe out the enemy."

"*I'll* stay here!" I fired a string of shots as I spoke.

"Cut it out! Carry out the battle plan. Hurry!"

His words carried authority. How could I compare my ability to command with his? I led Platoon Two and the artillery platoon crawling away from the fire fight. Once clear, we jumped up and closely followed the point platoon forward.

Liang and Platoon Three did not catch up with us until ten o'clock. As he wiped away sweat and gunpowder smoke from his face with his sleeve he told me with grief that two of his soldiers had been killed and one wounded, and that the martyrs' bodies and the wounded had been left to the vice-instructor, who had been assigned that duty.

The mountain area of northern Vietnam is overgrown with tall weeds and dense bushes. The slopes are steep and there are few paths through them. The bamboo stalks grow thick as drinking mugs and, bunched together in groves, form a natural barrier that cannot be cut through or pushed aside. The cogon grass grows more than two meters high. Entwined all through the cogon are low shrubs with long, thorny vines, which made passage virtually impossible. Even though the lunar half-month rain water had just ended, the temperature was already getting as high as 34 to 35° centigrade. All of these factors brought us unimaginable difficulties during our rapid forward thrust.

We were pushing ahead impatiently along the valley when the point platoon stopped. I went up to the front and looked out upon an expanse of cassava forest, each tree over three meters wide and two meters high. It was too dense to move through and too brittle for a human to step on. Jin Kailai swung his Dai broadsword, now here, now there, cutting a path for the whole company. Meanwhile, the battalion commander called over the walkie-talkie to check on Company Nine's current location. Liang Sanxi hurriedly unfolded the map and scanned the detailed lines. A soldier carrying an 8.2 recoilless cannon on his shoulder moved next to Liang Sanxi. He quickly scanned the map, then pointed to a coordinate and said, "Sure

. . . here—this is Company Nine's position."

Liang Sanxi nodded. He looked over this soldier who had just been sent to us as a reinforcement, then reported Company Nine's position to the battalion commander through the walkie-talkie. The commander's voice came back anxiously. "Too slow! Too slow! Speed up your advance! You have to speed up your advance!"

"Yes!" answered Liang to the commander, then stood up and gave orders to the whole company: "Throw away all your field packs and unnecessary clothing. The point platoon will continue to open up a path. All comrades from Platoons Two and Three and the company headquarters will help the artillery platoon carry the ammunition!"

The soldiers immediately obeyed the order. There was never a doubt that Liang's decision was anything but correct. Each of the infantrymen had been carrying a load of more than sixty jin, and each artilleryman more than ninety jin. But to speed up our thrust we had to throw away anything that was not absolutely necessary. After that was settled, Liang Sanxi asked the soldier who had the remarkable ability to figure out our position on the map, "Which command did you come from?"

"Beijing Command."

"What's your name?"

"Well . . . it's kind of hard to remember names on short order. Of all the fifteen reinforcements, I'm the only one from Beijing Command, so why not just call me 'Beijing'?"

This soldier Beijing was tall and handsome. He seemed thoughtful, too, and brimmed with enthusiasm. When he winked his eyes under heavy brows he looked especially shrewd.

"All right. You march with me," said Liang Sanxi. Obviously, a capable soldier was exactly what Liang needed now.

We were able to speed up the thrust. Twice along one mountain ridge we engaged small pockets of enemy troops. Again, with Liang Sanxi leading Platoon Three and covering my retreat, we quickly threw off the enemy and thrust tooth and nail forward. The battalion commander checked our position over the walkie-talkie from time to time, and was always dissatisfied with our slow progress.

At 3:00 in the afternoon the commander radioed us again. Soldier Beijing quickly found our position on the map. After hearing Liang's report, the commander lost his temper. "The division and regimental commanders are extremely dissatisfied with your slow advance! Dissatisfied! If you don't reach the designated position in time, you'll be disciplined after the battle! Disciplined! Tell Zhao Mengsheng to come over and talk to me." Liang Sanxi moved over a bit to let me squat down.

"Zhao Mengsheng! Zhao Mengsheng!" said the battalion commander. "You know how you behaved before the battle. The corps commander has just asked me about your behavior. You should be careful! Be careful! Political agitation is a serious matter. Serious! They must not think that you are lax in political agitation. Pay attention, or *you* will not speak for yourself after the battle!" I felt my scalp tingle. Liang Sanxi pushed me aside to talk again.

"Comrade Battalion Commander, the political agitation is important . . . important. But we don't have time to chat! Do you have any instructions? Say them!"

"Liang Sanxi, don't be stubborn! Wartime discipline is merciless on anyone!"

The battalion commander had no sooner stopped shouting than Jin Kailai, who had just returned from the point platoon, began to complain. "Dammit! They can execute their wartime discipline! Shoot us dead. Let them shoot us all dead! The only thing they know is how to measure maps with rulers. Are we advancing along a straight line? Let them come and look and tell me if human beings can climb this mountain. The path—that's what I want to know! Where is the path for us mere humans to walk on?"

"Vice-Commander, stop complaining!" The veins on Liang's temples were throbbing.

Jin Kailai became silent.

Liang Sanxi commanded in a stern voice to all, "Take good care of your weapons and ammunition. Each soldier: keep marching rations for two meals and your canteen—do not ever lose your canteen—and throw away all the rest."

No one who has not personally experienced warfare could imagine the terrible position we were in as the advance company in this thrust. In order to get to the designated position on time we had to hack our way through the subtropical mountain jungle while we endured the blazing heat of the sun. We risked our lives simply to climb up each hill. We slid and stumbled our way downhill. Our clothes were torn to shreds. Our bodies turned black and blue.

After sunset everything around us seemed to loom above us in the darkness. I could no longer discern our direction. I pulled my stiff legs forward and struggled to stay up with the others. When I heard Liang Sanxi say that we had arrived at the designated position, I immediately collapsed.

Liang Sanxi helped me back up and walked me a bit. I pulled myself together, then saw that most of the other soldiers were lying on the ground. Still propping me up, Liang gave orders: "Get up! Help your comrades move their legs and arms." Suddenly he loosened his grip on me, and called in a low voice: "Xiao . . . Jin, Xiao Jin!"

I saw Xiao Jin, the bugler, fall facedown in the grass. Liang Sanxi began to shake him. "Xiao Jin! Jin Xiaozhu . . . . " Xiao Jin made no response. Liang Sanxi and I hurriedly unloaded Xiao Jin's gear—a submachine gun, cartridge belt, twelve hand grenades, a bugle with its red tassel, two packs of hardtack, and a canteen. On top of that, he was carrying four heavy 8.2 recoilless cannon shells. You could see that he had obeyed the company commander's orders and relieved the artillery platoon soldiers of theirs.

Liang Sanxi sat down on the ground and leaned Xiao Jin against his arm. He picked up Xiao Jin's canteen and shook it. There was still some water in it. He put the open end to Xiao Jin's mouth and said, "Xiao Jin, wake up. Have some water . . . . "

Xiao Jin made no movement, his mouth still tightly shut.

I administered artificial respiration, but it was no use. His heart had stopped beating.

Tears sprang from Liang Sanxi's eyes. He wiped the stains and sweat from Xiao Jin's face with a hand towel. Xiao Jin's long eyelashes went down, but two shallow dimples remained in his plump cheeks. Before he could sound the charge for the whole company—before he could kill the enemy and win any merit—he fell asleep serenely, and forever.

Later, I thought it over, time and again. If Xiao Jin had not tried to carry those four shells for the artillery platoon, then he might not have . . . . Maybe he was too young. Or maybe something had been wrong with his heart or something else inside. The forced march was more than he could bear. This soldier who was not even seventeen died of overexertion on the battlefield.

Now I held his pudgy hands and cried. It was this pair of hands that had brought water every morning for me to wash my face, and even squeezed toothpaste over my toothbrush. It was this pair of hands that had diligently washed my uniforms. This pair of hands had helped me back to my feet when I collapsed during the full-dress, ten-kilometer cross-country march. My age was almost twice his, yet I thought, "Forgive me, Xiao Jin. I won't be an inexperienced political instructor forever. And I will never be a traitor, either."

In war, time is usually reckoned in minutes and seconds. It was already 20.02 when we arrived at the forward position of Height 364. We were 122 minutes behind schedule.

Nobody in Company Nine needed to have any regrets about that.

Seven

Liang Sanxi gave orders for an equipment check. No weapons or ammunition had been lost. However, most of the men had thrown their canteens and rations away during the forward march. Liang told each platoon to gather up whatever rations and water were left. After everyone had eaten the common meal, Communist-style, there were hardly any food rations or water left in the whole company.

I had thrown my canteen and rations away, but I wouldn't accept the half package of hardtack that Liang offered me. I told him I still had something to eat. Then Liang insisted that I take the canteen Xiao Jin had left, but how could I bear to drink Xiao Jin's water? I handed Xiao Jin's canteen and his four cannon shells over to the artillery platoon.

The nighttime sky was as dark as a boundless, bottomless abyss.

Inside a stand of shrubs at the foot of a cliff, Liang Sanxi called together all the squad and platoon leaders to plan the next operation. He opened his map in the darkness. With the glowing dot of a pen light, Liang pointed at Height 364, which was made up of a higher peak and an unnamed hill, and asked our guide, the repatriated Chinese, to tell us about the enemy's fortifications on the height.

The guide was a farmer, about thirty-four or thirty-five. During the thrust, two of our strongest soldiers who were not carrying anything else had to prop him up. That was the only thing that kept him from falling behind. He had come back to China when the Vietnamese government turned on us and started to discriminate against the Chinese there. He used to live near Height 364. The sad thing was that he hardly knew anything about the enemy's military deployment. All he could tell us was that he had seen the Vietnamese soldiers putting up blockhouses and defense works on the higher peak and the unnamed hill in front of his home since the spring of 1974. That was it.

Since we had already squared off against the elaborately constructed defenses on Height 364, we focused our thoughts. Liang Sanxi was already thinking of the new soldier, Beijing, as the company's staff officer. Now he said to Beijing next to him, "Comrade Beijing, you tell us what you think."

"All right. I'll tell you what I have in my underdeveloped mind so you can build on it with better ideas," said Beijing. "It is our company alone that is in the enemy's heart, far away from our base camp. It will be very difficult to occupy the higher peak and unnamed hill in front of us without strong gunfire cover. The enemy holds the high ground and they could guess we're worn out. As the saying goes, 'One man defending the right position can hold off ten thousand enemies.' The circumstances have determined our attack for us: use strategy rather than take by storm."

"Seems reasonable," Liang Sanxi said and urged him to go on.

"We've run out of food and water, and we're not going to get any more anytime soon. So we have to strike fast. I say we start fighting tonight instead of tomorrow, before the enemy can even locate us. And we begin with a little prologue."

"A prologue?" asked Liang Sanxi.

Beijing continued. "Yes. Sun Tzu in *The Art of War* wrote, 'Know the enemy and know yourself. You can fight a hundred battles with no danger of defeat.' My little prologue would be first to get past the mine field by clearing out a path so the whole company can get right up to the enemy. Then, with the infantry platoons firing to draw out the enemy fire—that would help us locate their positions—the artillery platoon and the demolition teams from infantry can close in on them in the dark. With good cover they can reach the enemy's firing positions. The nearer, the better. Then, at daybreak, we capture the unnamed hill as quick as lightning and we gain a foothold. We can't even consider the next step until then."

I was surprised at how well this soldier Beijing was versed in military tactics. He completely convinced me. We all discussed the plan for a while in low voices, and agreed that Beijing's scheme was feasible.

After that, Beijing said "I have been a soldier in the 8.2 recoilless artillery squad, infantry company, since I enlisted. While I was in the Beijing Region Command I took part in some assault drills in a mountainous area, using live ammunition. When you need something to destroy the enemy's firing points at close range, the 8.2 recoilless cannon is it. Its effective range is 1,000 meters. The unique thing is that you can use the mouth of the cannon like a bayonet if you shoulder it and aim straight. In hilly terrain, any rock can be your cover. I have shot from my shoulder many times within 100 meters of the target. You don't even have to aim. Every shot hit the target, as if you were aiming straight into the enemy's belly. So now we're going to charge enemy positions in a mountainous area. If we choose long-distance firing, one shell falling short could sacrifice our charging infantry. I also think 4.0 rocket launchers should be launched within a distance of 100 meters, or even 50 meters! Every shot must score. We must never play down those Vietnamese soldiers. They've had years of experience in battle, and they'll do anything to get what they want. In the end, we've got to take big risks and beat them our way."

Liang Sanxi said "what Beijing is saying is very reasonable. When we fire the 8.2 recoilless cannon and launch the 4.0 rockets we have to get in as close as possible. Each shell has to wipe out a blockhouse. Otherwise . . . you all know what will happen. Leader of Platoon One: the move will still start with your point platoon. You'll have to detonate the enemy's mines first. Use bundles of hand grenades."

By this time, Jin Kailai had lost patience. "Dammit! Let's get a move on. Tie up ten bundles of hand grenades first, each one with ten pieces."

Liang Sanxi pushed him down and set about making the detailed battle assignments. After that, Liang said to me, "Instructor, if we move the battle starting time forward, we would ordinarily report it to the battalion. But using the walkie-talkie right under the enemy's nose would mean giving away our position. What do you think?"

I said without hesitation, "There's no need to report anything. We have to capture the two peaks sooner or later. Sooner is always better than later."

Beijing added, "Instructor's word is quite right. A general commanding during battle does not have to accept orders even from his emperor."

The operation began.

The point platoon led by Jin Kailai threw the hand grenades bundle after bundle over the mine field. The explosion of the grenades was instantly echoed by the explosion of mines. Braving the smarting smoke of the TNT, the whole company low-crawled over the blasted route through the mine field, rapidly and safely.

By this time Platoon Three, in charge of the firepower decoy, had begun shooting with light and heavy machine guns. Tongues of fire spewed out from the enemy's scattered firing points on the unnamed hill. Suddenly, the crack of gunfire was heard everywhere.

I quietly counted the enemy firing points and said to Liang Sanxi, "Twelve. There are twelve points in all."

"No. More than that. At least thirteen."

According to the division of troops we had made before the fight, Liang Sanxi and I each led two squads of the artillery platoon and the demolition teams from the infantry platoons. We inched our way forward up both sides of the unnamed hill to cover near the enemy's blockhouses.

Jin Kailai went with me. Having him at my side helped me keep myself together. Now this vice-company commander from the artillery platoon, carrying a rocket launcher in his hand and rocket shells on his back, was raring to go and blast the blockhouses.

Platoon Three's light and heavy machine guns rattled from time to time, as did the weapons from the enemy's different blockhouses. The tongues of fire betrayed their origins, allowing us to take action.

I was crawling forward when Jin Kailai gave a pull at my clothes and whispered, "Keep calm. You just follow me!"

Closer. The blockhouses spewing the tongues of fire grew closer and closer.

At midnight, the unnamed hill completely quieted down.

Jiu, jiu . . . jiji, jiji. Katydids, golden beetles, crickets, and other insects whose names I could never guess performed soft serenades. Jin Kailai and I lay next to each other in the thick cogon grass at the foot of a cliff. He was a man who never could stand silence. He asked me in my ear, "Instructor, what are you thinking about?"

"I . . . nothing."

"Don't you miss your wife?" he blurted out.

"Right now, I'm not in a position to think about her."

"Your wife must be beautiful. Is she Western-style?"

"A bit. But, maybe country women are more sincere."

After a few minutes, he muttered again, "My little boy is four years old. He's me all over again. His birthday is next month, the sixth. How I hope to hold him in my arms and kiss him on the cheek."

We both closed our eyes to pull ourselves together. It wasn't until then I noticed that my uniform, which had gotten soaked with sweat over and over again, was now as hard as armor. My legs were as heavy and stiff as two logs. A scorching pain racked my whole body.

We heard the ring of a telephone overhead. Then came shouts and a brouhaha. Ah! Enemy soldiers in the blockhouse were making a telephone call. My nerves shrank and my fatigue disappeared immediately.

Here, right under the enemy's blockhouse, I understood so deeply that there wasn't any difference between a general's son and a farm boy. We would endure the thunder and endure the fire with the same human bodies. We would greet Death. We would fight Death. We would write down news of victory for our homeland with our warm blood!

Eight

The morning mist, at first as thick as gauze, softly dissipated with the first glimmer of dawn in the east. With three red signal flares streaming high into the sky, Liang Sanxi signalled the charge.

Jin Kailai at my side had already jumped to his feet. He leaned against a rock, a rocket launcher on his shoulder, and pulled the trigger in an instant. With a boom, one of the blockhouses blew sky high before it could spew out another tongue of fire.

At almost the same instant, Beijing, who was more than 30 meters away from me, shouldered his 8.2 caliber recoilless cannon. His body shuddered as a snake-like flame spurted out from behind his shoulder.

"Take cover, Instructor!" At Jin Kailai's shout I fell flat behind a rock. Pieces of the blockhouse rained down around me.

The thundering rumbled nonstop. The smoke from gunfire rolled here and there up the unnamed hill. Things seemed to be going very smoothly for Liang Sanxi's troops, who were attacking from the left flank.

Jin Kailai and Beijing rushed forward while their support, led by myself, moved quickly into the rocky area where we could safely cover them. Now, flames were shooting out of the two blockhouses that stood on the upper right side of the unnamed hill.

I gave the command to fire. My cover squad fired in unison, drawing enemy fire back on us.

Jin Kailai and Beijing, each shouldering a weapon, outflanked two sides of both blockhouses at a distance of about 50 meters. It was as if they were using their launcher and cannon as bayonets. With two thundering crashes, two more blockhouses blew into the air.

As soon as the thunder ended, all of us pounced on the unnamed hill like so many hungry tigers. Liang Sanxi, who had attacked from the left flank, reached the hill simultaneously.

The enemy put up a last-ditch effort, but all of them who didn't run away were gunned down. There was no time to shout in Vietnamese "*Nor song kon yie*" (Lay down your arms!) or "*Zoun tui kuan hong du bing.*" (We give lenience to prisoners.)

The battle lasted barely ten minutes, and it was neatly won.

Liang Sanxi slapped Beijing on the shoulder in excitement. "Well done! You're really our backbone from Beijing. You're going to be the first one we recommend for a citation after this is over." Then he gave orders to the whole company. "Everyone: clear up this battlefield and get into the trench. We've got to hold it now against an enemy counterattack!"

We all quickly piled into the trench and prepared for their counterattack to retake the trench. I had not yet realized that the battle was actually going into a more brutal stage. The unnamed hill itself was held by a reinforced enemy company. The enemy's battalion headquarters and a 120-mortar platoon occupied the highest peak. We didn't find this out until after the battle was over.

Enemy troops on the highest peak began to pelt the unnamed hill with gunfire. Shells whistled in and exploded along the trench that we had captured. Smoke enveloped us like a vast, black gauze so dense that neither sun nor sky could penetrate. Earth, stones, and firearms abandoned by the enemy all jumped frantically to the zinging of flying shrapnel.

Between each volley of gunfire the enemy charged from three directions. Because we held the vantage point, we had quickly repulsed the first two counterattacks. But our company had already suffered casualties, eleven wounded and eight dead.

The enemy's third charge came after a particularly frantic bombardment. Jin Kailai and I both picked up light machine guns and held down the western edge of the position with Platoon One. More than thirty Vietnamese troops, covered by gunfire, charged at us in small groups, shouting and screaming.

We sprayed the enemy with gunfire but the time between the three charges was too short. Before long, our machine gun barrels were so red that we had to stop firing.

"Get me the hand grenades. Hurry! The more the better!" Jin Kailai threw his cap aside, exposing his shaved head. Fortunately for us this position that the enemy had abandoned was cluttered with firearms and even some ammunition crates that were still sealed—everything stamped *Made in China*. I dragged up a crate of hand grenades and handed him a few.

"Screw the caps off! Screw all the caps off for me!" roared Jin Kailai, throwing the first grenades. "Change your firearms. Hurry!"

Having a true warrior like Jin Kailai stay right in the thick of it with us was enough to turn a coward brave. Clinging to life had no place here. It was far better to fight tooth and nail than to die a craven death. I unscrewed the cap off each grenade one by one for Jin Kailai, who was throwing them with both hands. This gave our soldiers time to change their firearms.

The enemy's bullets poured upon us like a swarm of locusts. As more soldiers took hits their bodies fell against the trench wall. All of us were risking getting shot a hundred times every minute.

This, then, is War!—where one may encounter every experience and emotion, imaginable and otherwise, in a few hours, or in a few minutes, experiences that others may never know after a lifetime, no matter how old a noncombatant may live. Victory or defeat, hope or despair, excitement or sorrow, life—or death in a twinkling. War distills all of these with its own ferocity.

We smashed the enemy for the third time, leaving heaps of bodies strewn in front of our position. The enemy stopped shelling from the highest peak. The battlefield quieted down.

Jin Kailai and I located Liang Sanxi in the center of the trench. He had bandaged his left arm, probably taking a hit during the enemy's third attack. We went over to see about his wound, but he gave a shake of his arm and said, "No matter so far. The bullet went through without hitting the bone."

Soldiers laid the bodies of the martyrs in the trench. I estimated that we had lost about a third of Company Nine.

Nobody had any tears left to shed. We had gotten so used to blood and the death of our comrades that not much else could bring sorrow to us. There was room for only one thought in our minds—*revenge*.

Liang Sanxi happened to see Duan Yuguo from Squad Three, sprawled along the ground, his torso held in the arms of his squad leader. Liang asked, "Why . . . was Xiao Duan wounded?"

"No," said the squad leader. "He passed out from thirst. He's not half bad. He blew up a blockhouse all by himself when we led our charge at dawn."

"Well, he's not a coward after all," said Liang Sanxi with a note of praise.

We sat down. Liang Sanxi handed his half canteen of water to the squad leader. "Let him drink all of it. Hurry."

The squad leader wouldn't have it, and Liang Sanxi got angry. "Don't waste time on the battlefield."

Slowly the squad leader poured the water into Duan Yuguo's mouth, until the young soldier came to. The squad leader told him, "That was the company commander's water, the only half canteen of water left in Company Nine."

Duan Yuguo opened his eyes slowly and gazed at Liang, his lips quivering, his tears falling down from his cheeks.

Between the enemy's attacks, Liang Sanxi had sent soldiers around the unnamed hill to look for water and food. The only source of water was a well beside the enemy's barracks, and, according to the medic's chemical analysis, that had been poisoned. The barracks that the enemy had abandoned still held grain sacks marked "RICE OF CHINA." But what use was rice without water?

The sun was scorching at noon. We were smothering under the heat. The Squad Three leader glanced at Liang Sanxi and me, and said with a halt, "There was a . . . a patch of sugar cane at the foot of the hill . . . . "

Jin Kailai stretched out his hand toward me, as if he hadn't heard the squad leader's words. "Instructor, have you got a cigarette? Damn it all, mine got lost yesterday during the forward thrust."

I shook my head. I had taken two cartons with me when we set off, but I had thrown them away during the thrust.

Liang Sanxi took out his Hongtashan. There were only two left. He handed one to Jin Kailai and shared the other one with me. Jin Kailai lit up, took two greedy drags and said, "Instructor, may I go bring back something to fortify us?"

I knew what he meant by "something to fortify," so I stood up. "Let me go with a few soldiers. We'll get a bundle of it."

Jin Kailai stood up, too, and pressed me back down. "It's not your turn to go, but I'm glad to hear you volunteer. How could I let you, the political instructor, violate the principle? Me—Jin Kailai—I'm famous for having no political sense. I'd rather go back to my hometown under disciplinary punishment after this is over than die of thirst . . . if I don't get killed first."

Before the battle, the commanding officer had repeatedly stressed the military principles: within the Vietnamese border, nothing could be taken from civilians, not even a single needle or piece of thread. Violators would be doubly punished.

Then Jin Kailai started to complain. "Us poor people had to tighten our belts so we could give away twenty billion yuan to them. God dammit! Why shouldn't we trade twenty billion yuan for a bundle of sugar cane?" Finishing that, he turned to the leader of Squad Three. "Take your squad and come with me." He jumped out of the trench and led the men away.

Liang Sanxi and I wearily trudged along the trench checking the status of squad after squad, platoon after platoon. We saw three more wounded soldiers die of thirst or hemorrhage. Those who survived were suffering from extreme dehydration as they rested against the trench wall under the scorching sun. They hardly had the strength to speak.

We were dying of thirst. *Water* was what we needed to "fortify" us. Liang Sanxi could not stand up any longer, and sat down with me. Leaning against the trench, he let out a long sigh.

Suddenly a thundering explosion roared from downhill, to the right. Thinking that the enemy was taking trial shots to gauge our range before the next bombardment, we jumped up, ordered the soldiers to take their battle positions, and prepared to fight back. But nothing happened.

In a few minutes, the Squad Three leader, carrying a large bundle of sugar cane on his shoulder, rushed into the trench.

"It was horrible! Vice-Commander Jin stepped on a mine as we were coming back. He . . . he always insists on going ahead of everyone else when we go out. He . . . . " The squad leader wept loudly.

Soon the soldiers of Squad three carried Jin Kailai to the edge of the trench. Liang and I carried him on into it. We laid him out on the ground. His left foot was blasted away, and his whole body was covered with wounds. We hurriedly dressed the wounds.

He turned toward us in great agony and pushed us away. "No. I don't need any bandages . . . . I'm . . . dying. You all . . . come over here . . . to eat . . . this sugar cane . . . . "

"Vice-Commander, you . . . . " Liang Sanxi flung himself onto Jin Kailai and began sobbing.

Jin Kailai stroked Liang's shoulder and said, "Commander, take good care of yourself. It doesn't matter about me. I have three brothers . . . . "

"Vice-Commander . . . " I whimpered.

He turned to me. "Instructor, I'm a roughneck . . . . Spit it out: you forgive me . . . . "

"Vice-Commander . . . " I cried out loudly.

With great difficulty, he pointed to his left breast pocket. "Instructor, take it out for me . . . . No, not a notebook full of brave words. It's a picture of my whole family . . . . "

I put my hand into his pocket and took out a photograph of Jin Kailai, his wife, and a boy about four years old.

I had tears in my eyes when I showed him the photo. He took it with his trembling hand. "I'm . . . going . . . let me . . . have a last look . . . . "

Zhao Mengsheng was choked with sobs, unable to go on.

After a while he swept off his tears and said to me, "Then Vice-Commander Jin Kailai died. When I think of him now, it isn't his death that gets to me . . . . "

Duan Yuguo stepped in. "After we got back inside China, Instructor Zhao had repeatedly asked the regiment command to cite the Vice-Commander for his meritorious service. But he never got them to award Jin Kailai any citation, not even a Third Class Merit."

Zhao Mengsheng continued. "Vice-Commander could have earned the title Combat Hero, if his heroism had been taken into account. He really could have been propagandized if he had died with a notebook full of brave words in his pocket. But when we filed a report with regiment headquarters about his heroism on the battlefield—the whole truth—someone at regiment said, 'Jin Kailai was a big complainer who never had a great thought in his life. Before the battle, when he was promoted to vice-company commander, he said he had been asked to die before the others. What's more, he died for a bundle of sugar canes. That not only seriously violated military discipline, but also made his death pointless!'"

"*No!* Worthy. His death was absolutely worthy!" Duan Yuguo shouted. "Everyone gets demerits. Jin Kailai didn't complain without good reason. We don't care what anyone else says. Vice Commander Jin will forever be a great hero for the men in Company Nine. If we hadn't gotten that bundle of sugar cane, we would all have passed out from thirst. How would we have captured the highest peak!"

We each became silent.

After a long pause, Zhao Mengsheng heaved a deep sigh and went on with the description of the second half of the battle.

Nine

The fierce battle grew fiercer.

We had no sooner chewed up our allotment of two pieces of sugar cane before the enemy launched a downward bombardment from the highest peak—more frenzied, more violent than the last one. It went on for half an hour. Our trench, which we had used as a foothold on the unnamed hill, was pocked all around with shell craters. The smoke of gunpowder was so strong that we couldn't open our eyes, and the stench of the TNT took our breath away.

As soon as the bombardment ended, their antiaircraft machine guns and light and heavy machine guns all spewed out fire and bullets onto the unnamed hill from the two blockhouses halfway up the highest peak. It was obvious that the enemy intended to start another counterattack from the south.

"Platoon Three, neutralize the enemy's fire!" Liang Sanxi shouted.

We had just stuck our heads out of the trench when we saw a cluster of enemy troops climbing over the cliff in front of our trench, hardly more than thirty feet in front of us.

"Fire!"

With his shout, Liang Sanxi took up his light machine gun and fired into the enemy. The rest of the company rallied the strength to open fire. Within seconds, the enemy's sneak attack was repelled. They fled in panic.

The enemy had come down from the highest peak during the bombardment when we couldn't watch everything that was going on. They climbed through the gap between the highest peak and the unnamed hill, and mounted their sneak attack on our forward position. If we had discovered them a few seconds later, they would have swarmed into our trench.

After the rout, both sides were quiet again.

A while later, the telegraph operator ran up to Liang Sanxi, saying that the battalion commander was asking for Company Nine over the walkie-talkie. Liang Sanxi briefly reported in to the battalion commander on the course of events in capturing the unnamed hill. The battalion commander told us over the walkie-talkie that the other three companies in our battalion were still ten kilometers away from the unnamed hill. The original plan for the assault was by now completely muddled. Each company at the moment held a main mountain pass in order to intercept enemy troops routed from the first defense line. That would take care of any enemy troops trying to escape. But it also meant that none of our battalion troops could be released to reinforce our position on the unnamed hill. The battalion commander said he wanted to withdraw the criticism he made yesterday, and instead transmitted divisional and regimental citations to Company Nine, saying that the speed of our thrust yesterday had been amazingly fast.

Yes. If they had walked along the path we cut yesterday, they would have understood why Company Nine was 122 minutes off schedule.

"Difficulty: have you any difficulty?" asked the battalion commander.

"Over one-third dead or wounded, and we've run out of food and water!" Liang Sanxi shouted. "Water! We have an urgent need for water."

"Stand firm! You must try to hold out until tomorrow morning, when we'll be able to climb up the unnamed hill." The battalion commander paused, then shouted, "The regimental commanders instruct that if you have difficulty in capturing the highest peak, you can stick to the unnamed hill until we get there."

"No. We could never stick to the unnamed hill! If we're going to die, we'd rather die on the highest peak."

"What? Are you Liang Sanxi or Jin Kailai? What's all the complaining?"

"Reporting! This is Liang Sanxi. Jin Kailai is dead," said Liang, his face turning livid. "There's an enemy mortar position on the highest peak and it's constantly pouring gunfire on us. Company Nine would be completely wiped out before tomorrow morning if we stayed here."

Liang Sanxi signed off with the battalion commander and then said to me, "Instructor, shouldn't we hold a Party member meeting?" I informed the Party members that we were going to meet. Some non-Party members asked if they could join in. Liang and I were soon surrounded by Party members and nonmembers.

Liang Sanxi said, "I'm afraid that we're going to stall out if we stay in this position. We have to regain the initiative by launching an attack. We could make up a shock team of Party members to go and take the highest peak and occupy the enemy's mortar position."

Beijing picked up on the idea. "What Company Commander said is a pretty good idea. It looks like the enemy's military forces on the highest peak aren't all that strong—except for the mortars, which is what they've been relying on to inflict these heavy losses on us. We— here in Company Nine—are never going to be secure until we are standing on the enemy's mortar position ourselves."

Liang Sanxi glanced over the people around him and then pronounced two orders. "I'm appointing the artillery platoon leader to be acting vice-company commander. I'm also appointing Beijing as acting artillery platoon leader." The artillery platoon leader had replaced Jin Kailai just before the battle. Then he asked me, "We don't have time for a discussion. What do you think about the plan, Instructor?"

I nodded my agreement. Getting promotions on this battlefield didn't need any backdoor deals. The men took their new posts when the time came, or as Jin Kailai had put it, they were assigned to die first.

Beijing then said to Liang Sanxi, "I'm not going to be modest, not now, Commander. The fact is I'm really pretty good at leading an artillery platoon. But I'm great at blowing up blockhouses with an 8.2 recoilless cannon. I think I'd do a better job as an artilleryman."

Thinking that the request sounded reasonable, Liang Sanxi nodded his approval. A shock team of Party and League members was formed. Liang Sanxi decided on the spot that the team would be led by the new vice-commander and himself, and they would attack the highest peak from opposite sides. I was to stay on the unnamed hill with Platoon Three to cover their attack.

"Commander, you've been wounded in the arm!" I protested. "If you don't think I'm a coward, let me lead the shock team."

"That's nonsense! Everybody on this battlefield saw whether or not you're a coward," said Liang Sanxi. The look in his eyes showed that he was not going to argue. "You're just not qualified to take command. All right, before the next bombardment starts we've got to make every second count." He turned to Beijing and waved him forward. "You and the ammunition men get down the slope first with enough shells. The faster the better."

Between the unnamed hill and the highest peak there was a U-shaped pass. The slope in front of our position ran down at a 70-degree angle. It was well within enemy range and exposed to enemy fire. The moment Beijing rushed down the slope with his 8.2 recoilless cannon, followed by the ammunition carriers, enemy troops in the blockhouses halfway up the highest peak began to rake their path with a shower of bullets.

"Platoon Three, draw off the enemy fire!" Liang Sanxi ordered.

Platoon Three opened fire on the blockhouses but the sly enemy ignored the ploy and kept firing on the slope in front of us. It was going to be horrible getting down that open slope inside enemy range.

Liang Sanxi furrowed his brows. After a moment he shouted out at the shock team members, "Look at me! Do what I do!"

Finishing the sentence, he picked up a light machine gun and nimbly jumped out of the trench between bursts of enemy gunfire and rolled swiftly down the slope.

I was astonished. As a commander 'at the critical moment,' he mustered all his loyalty, bravery, and wisdom, and turned them into this resolute and brave action. He succeeded. The shock team members, following his example between bursts of gunfire, tumbled out of the trench one after the other, and swiftly rolled themselves down the slope.

The firing stopped after a while. When things had quieted down again, I started to feel upset. I asked myself, *Didn't you vow to wipe out your humiliation? Then why don't you follow Liang Sanxi's example and charge forward?* The enemy's blanket firing started up again. I grabbed a submachine gun and shouted to Platoon Three, "You stick to the position. I'm going down there."

I hurried out of the trench, lay down, and rolled downhill with all my might. What I focused on was that we are all human beings born to our parents. Whatever Liang Sanxi could do, I as an instructor should be able to do. Strange to say, when I was rolling down the mountain, I didn't feel any pain, just numbness all over my body.

The highest peak was covered with palm grass that grew as tall as a man. As soon as I got into the grass, I was out of the enemy's firing blanket. I quickly crawled forward and caught up with Liang Sanxi and the soldiers. Liang did not scold me when he saw me. Platoon Three was still shooting at the enemy, who was still firing back. We climbed uphill through the thick grass to get nearer the blockhouses. After a long crawl, we could see the blockhouses by peeking over the tops of the palm grass.

Beijing said to Liang Sanxi, "Commander, they're fifty meters away at most. I guarantee I won't need a second shot. Come on."

Liang nodded.

Beijing put a shell into the bore. A moment later, the 8.2 recoilless cannon poised on his shoulder, he jumped up and pressed the trigger. There was no trail of fire! Beijing quickly dropped to the ground. Enemy bullets whistled over our heads.

"What's wrong? A dud?" asked Liang Sanxi.

"Yeah. A bad one," said Beijing, and unloaded the dud shell. An ammunition carrier passed another shell over to Beijing, who loaded it in the cannon. After another short pause, Beijing shouldered the cannon and jumped up again. He pulled the trigger but *again* there was no trail of fire!

The enemy's guns rattled. At the sound of shooting, Beijing was thrown down on the ground.

"Beijing! Comrade Beijing—" shouted Liang Sanxi and I. It had all happened in a second.

Beijing lay in a pool of blood. He had taken seven bullets from the antiaircraft machine gun, each bullet hole big as a shot glass and gushing warm blood.

He had fallen, an outstanding soldier who never even had time to groan before he died. He made his farewell to life in his early twenties when he had a great future awaiting him. He was so capable, so talented. Only yesterday the fight plan that he had figured out had helped us capture the unnamed hill. In a second he was cut down. It was only two days since he had hurried to the front from Beijing Command and been sent as a reinforcement to our company. We didn't even know his real name. From a distance of fifty meters he couldn't have missed hitting a blockhouse. He didn't even have to aim. But the faulty shells! Two damned faulty shells!

Liang Sanxi glared at the ammunition carrier crawling toward him. "You're responsible for his death!"

The ammunition carrier hung his head silently. I knew that Liang Sanxi was too grieved to control himself. He was venting his rage. In this life-and-death battle, with all of us facing the same fate, who would have wanted two bad shells?

"How could we get two dud shells in a row?"

"This morning, during the attack on the unnamed hill, there had already been one dud," replied the ammunition carrier in grief. "If you want to know why they were duds, the registration on the casing will tell you."

Liang Sanxi picked up the first dud shell from the pool of blood under Beijing's body, had a look, then passed it to me. I located the registration marks on the side: Made in April, 1974.

The ammunition carrier muttered, "That stuff made during the Cultural Revolution—how *could* it be any good? Forget about production; political criticism was all anybody thought about then, even the munitions workers!"

I shuddered to think of that time of troubles, when the casualties included peoples' minds, and our national defense was wounded by armaments made so shoddy they don't even work. Now, on this battlefield of life and death, we were suffering the disastrous consequences of those dud shells.

"God damn it!" Liang Sanxi began to curse like Jin Kailai. "If those people go on scrambling for power and heaping criticism on each other—even on Confucius of two thousand years ago!—then we'll cave in on ourselves. No one will have to attack."

A thundering came from over on the left side of the peak. The new vice-commander and his soldiers had obviously blown up one of the blockhouses. The guns from the blockhouse above us started firing again. The spray of bullets zinged over our heads. Liang Sanxi asked the ammunition carrier, "How many shells do we still have?"

The man answered, "Nine—and six of them were made in April, 1974."

"Shit! Throw them away. Throw the six shells away!" In great anger Liang Sanxi said to the ammunition man sternly, "Be quick! Bring me a good one."

Liang Sanxi retrieved the blood-stained 8.2 recoilless cannon from under Beijing's body, unloaded the faulty shell and threw it away angrily. He took the good one from the ammunition carrier and loaded it into the cannon.

Liang Sanxi raised the cannon to his shoulder. With a sudden jerk of his body, a flame shot out of the muzzle. Then the shell exploded and the blockhouse was blown to pieces.

We jumped up even as the broken stones and dust were still raining down. We charged forward into the blast of gunpowder.

We made it to the top of the hill! The shock team stood poised at both sides. Infantry Platoon One, positioned at the face of the peak and now shouting and screaming, charged up to the hilltop.

At last, we stood on top of the highest peak of Height 364. At last!

"Watch out! Search for enemy remnants," Liang Sanxi ordered.

I looked around. Not a soul was to be seen in the disordered trench on the top of the highest peak. The mortar position to the right was cluttered with 120-mortars, the shells still stacked to be used. Heaps of sealed crates of shells lay all around. Now I was all the more convinced of the wisdom of Liang Sanxi's judgment. Without first capturing the mortar position, we would have been wiped out on the unnamed hill.

The hilltop was strewn with jagged rocks. We searched westward along the trench. Then Duan Yuguo ran up to Liang Sanxi and me excitedly. "Commander . . . Instructor . . . *victory!* We've won a victory at last! This battle could be written up as a pretty good drama!"

He looked so joyful. I never would have believed that he could have climbed the peak.

"Take cover! . . . " At Liang Sanxi's shout from behind us, a swift kick pushed me into the trench. The rattle of a machine gun followed.

When I looked over the trench again, I saw Liang Sanxi, our company commander, toppling down.

Without a second thought I threw myself at him. "Commander! Commander!" I sank to the ground and held him in my arms.

Liang Sanxi barely opened his eyes; he gripped his left breast pocket and said to me feebly, "Here . . . is a . . . list . . . of my debts . . . ."

Without finishing the sentence his head gently turned to the crook of my elbow. His body sank slowly, and his right hand gradually loosened its grip at the left breast pocket.

He had been hit in the left chest, just beside the heart—the most vital part of the human body. His face quickly sallowed.

"Commander! Commander!" The soldiers came hurrying, surrounding Liang Sanxi, some already weeping loudly.

"Commander!" Duan Yuguo flung himself on Liang Sanxi and wailed, "Commander, it's my fault . . . all my fault . . . . "

Nightmare! It was a nightmare. Liang Sanxi left us just as the battle was coming to its end! When the truth set in—that all this really had happened, quickly but undeniably, true as steel—I held Liang Sanxi tightly in my arms and burst into frantic tears.

Having said this, Zhao Mengsheng beat his head with both clenched hands, his eyes swimming with tears. His recounting had drawn him back into the horrible reality of the battle.

Immersed in Zhao's sorrow for Liang Sanxi's fate, I unconsciously wiped away my own tears.

After a long pause, Zhao Mengsheng raised his tear-stained face and mumbled to me, "The bullets were fired by a Vietnamese hiding behind rocks. Obviously, Liang Sanxi had discovered him first. If Liang hadn't given me that kick, he could have gotten out of the enemy's fire. It was for my sake that he . . . . "

Duan Yuguo was choking with sobs. He said guiltily, "It was my fault . . . my fault. I was dizzy with our success. Because I was celebrating our victory, Instructor wasn't paying attention to the danger of snipers, and Company Commander . . . . "

After a short while, Zhao Mengsheng continued.

"When I had pulled myself together, I recalled the sentence that Liang Sanxi had left unfinished. I found this note in the left breast pocket, next to the bleeding bullet hole . . . . "

Zhao Mengsheng drew out a piece of paper from a hard-bound notebook and handed it to me with a trembling hand. "You . . . have a look at this . . . . "

I took it from him. It was a blood-stained note that had been torn out of a small note pad. The words were hand-written boldly. Though stained with blood, the characters were still clearly discernible. The note read—

My Debts
Borrowed 120 yuan from the Company Quartermaster Section
Borrowed 70 yuan from Staff Sergeant Liu of Regiment Headquarters
Borrowed 40 yuan from Director Wang of the Regimental Logistics Department
Borrowed 50 yuan from Vice-Battalion Political Instructor Sun . . . .

The note detailed seventeen debts and creditors, and amounted to 620 yuan.

I felt a tingling in my scalp. Though I was still unaware of the reason why Liang Sanxi was head over heels in debt, it became clearer why Zhao Mengsheng had repeatedly referred to Liang Sanxi's frugal life in recounting Liang's story. Liang had smoked only black tobacco "gunpowder." His toothbrush only had eight tufts. He had never owned a watch.

Zhao Mengsheng heaved a sigh and said to me, "For more than three years this blood-stained debts list has weighed on me like one of those ancient millstones in the Yimeng mountains. Whenever I see it, mixed feelings well up in my heart. I often think of Liang Sanxi's unfinished sentence. It would have been, 'Here is a list of my debts, which I have not yet paid off. Not yet.'"

We sat in silence again. After a moment, I asked, "Then how did the battle end?"

Zhao Mengsheng was still weeping and made no answer.

Duan Yuguo said, "When I saw Company Commander shot down by a string of bullets, I thought he was taking cover by diving to the ground. I looked up and caught sight of a figure dashing away. I ran in that direction but saw nothing. Then some soldiers joined me in the search and we came to the opening of a cave at the bottom of the rocks. I turned back to tell Commander, but he had died in the arms of Instructor. I threw myself forward and burst into tears. When I told Instructor that the enemy had escaped into a cave, he jumped up in a frenzy and called out for hand grenades . . . ."

Zhao Mengsheng gestured for Duan Yuguo to stop. "Oh, come on. That's enough."

"But we have to tell what happened in the battle because the reporter has to write the story according to the facts." Duan Yuguo went on to tell me, "Instructor tied more than ten hand grenades together and ran headlong into the cave. Nobody could stop him. After a while we heard gunfire and then a muffled thunder. We were certain that Instructor had been killed. We made our way into the cave, each of us holding a flashlight. We carried Instructor out first. He was bleeding from a gash in the front and a wound in his back. He was unconscious. Then we pulled out nine dead bodies. The nine Vietnamese soldiers had been totally wiped out by Instructor's bundle of grenades! . . ."

"Enough. Stop pumping me up," Zhao Mengsheng said remorsefully. "Compared with Liang Sanxi, Jin Kailai, Beijing, and the bugler Xiao Jin, I was but a coward who had to be cursed and despised onto the battlefield by the corps commander and the comrades. If I can say that I am not ashamed of myself, it's because the spilt blood of the martyrs purified my spirit." He paused and gazed at me. "But what struck my heart most was not what happened on the battlefield, but what happened after the battle. It is a story that could move the heart of a statue, a story that I didn't expect then and that you could never guess now."

Ten

This was the only battle that Company Nine took part in.

The cave was pitch-dark when I entered it with the bundle of hand grenades. I could see nothing. I groped my way forward along the wall for more than ten meters before I began to hear sounds further inside. Of course, they heard me come in, and one of the enemy soldiers fired a volley of bullets, but he didn't hit me. I pulled the pins and threw the grenades at the enemy. Then I fell unconscious to the ground.

After that, the acting vice-company commander and his soldiers killed thirteen of the enemy in two more caves, like blocking up mouse holes. Then the battle was over: we had won.

I had been knocked unconscious by the explosion that I myself had caused. However, it wasn't a serious injury. Company Eight of our battalion soon replaced Company Nine on Height 364. I was first sent to the division field hospital, and then transferred back to China. I recovered about ten days later.

Then they withdrew our entire force from Vietnam. Huge crowds brought flowers and recited poetry for us in front of a triumphal arch. They gave us fine liquors at the victory banquet. But I became heavy-hearted whenever my thoughts returned to the martyrs who had sacrificed their lives.

Our troops started the process of merits appraisal. The corps headquarters decided to recommend to military command that Company Nine be awarded the title "Company Good at Attack and Defense." After discussions, the Party unit of Company Nine decided to recommend to the upper Party Committee that Liang Sanxi, Jin Kailai, and Beijing be awarded the title "Combat Hero." This decision would not have caused a bit of trouble if it hadn't included Jin Kailai. Ignoring the protests of Company Nine's Party unit, the regiment did not even award him a Third Class Merit. Then someone suggested that I be awarded the title "Combat Hero," saying that I had been the first one to get into the cave and blow up nine enemy soldiers singlehandedly—and that I could be described as a "Model Instructor." I was surrounded by popping flashbulbs and reporters lining up to talk to me.

The reporters seemed to be especially interested in me. Even my name attracted their attention. One reporter said I was worth the propaganda because I had been born on the Yimeng battlefield and now I had won merits on the battlefield for myself. To snatch the report for himself, he cornered me for an exclusive interview. He told me that he had even thought of a name for his news report. The headline would be "The General Raised a Successor"; the subhead would be "—Zhao Mengsheng, a hero growing up in a revolutionary family." He urged me to provide materials that would support his article. But I told him the truth straight out, which immediately threw in the wrench. Still, he persisted in propagandizing my story, and started to give a lot of rationalizations.

I absolutely refused. "If you want to write me up, you'll have to base your story on the truth, not on empty fluff."

That did it. The battle was barely over and the bodies of the martyrs were still warm. How could I decorate myself with the glory won by their blood?

Next, after the merits evaluation came the consolation for the families of martyrs. Our company had suffered the heaviest casualties in the whole regiment. The regiment command therefore had sent a special task force to help with this part.

The work went on smoothly enough. The martyrs' family members, deeply conscious of the righteousness of their husbands' and sons' sacrifice, made no claims beyond the stipulated compensations. What they wanted most was to know how their beloved men had died. One by one I told them of the meritorious deeds of the martyrs, and offered the medals conferred posthumously.

But when I stood in front of the widow and four-year-old boy of Jin Kailai, I was ashamed. I told her and her son how Vice-Commander Jin had led the point platoon to cut open a path for the whole company, about how he had blown up two enemy blockhouses, and how he had stuck to the unnamed hill to wipe out the enemy. I cut out the part about how he had led soldiers to get some sugarcane, saying only that Vice-Commander had stepped on a mine while looking for water along the front lines.

When Jin Kailai's widow looked up and gazed at me with her tearful eyes, I couldn't think of any words to comfort this contract worker of a commune cotton oil factory in Yu County, Henan Province. Every family of a martyr received a medal—mostly the Third-Class Merit—except her.

I wiped away my tears and pressed my medal of First-Class Merit into her hands. "Take it. This is the First-Class Medal that was conferred on Jin Kailai by Company Nine."

The simple and honest contract worker accepted the medal with both hands, wrapped it in a handkerchief along with the photo that Jin Kailai had left, and carefully put them away. She picked up her four-year-old boy and quietly went away.

Thank goodness for that! She didn't know that a company doesn't have the power to decide who should be awarded citations—not even a Third-Class Merit. I blessed her in my heart. I hoped the medal could relieve some small part of her great loss. I also hoped that the four-year-old boy, when he grew up, could at least be proud of his father, who had left him that medal.

The family members of the martyrs went away one by one, but Liang Sanxi's and Beijing's families were still nowhere to be seen. The regiment political department had both telegraphed and written to the civil administration department of Shandong Province asking them to inform Liang Sanxi's family to come to Company Nine. We also learned of Beijing's real name, Xue Kaihua, after we got back to China. The regimental section of military affairs had kept a list of all the reinforcements who had been rushed to the front from other military commands. Because they were so hurriedly assigned to each company, almost no outfit had found time to register their names. As a result, there were several companies that lost soldiers whose names were never known.

The three ranks of the Party committees—regiment, division, and corps—all decided to play up Liang Sanxi's heroic deeds for propaganda purposes, and asked us to collect items like photos, family letters, and recorded words of bravery that he might have left behind. The items were sent to the Heroic Deeds Exhibition presented by the military region command.

But we ran into difficulties in fulfilling their request. Except for the uniform overcoat that he had never worn, Liang Sanxi had left behind only two thread-bare uniforms. The regiment sent for both of the uniforms because the patches clearly showed that he always charged in the forefront of his soldiers, and that he took the lead in the all-company drills. The regiment also had heard about Liang Sanxi's toothbrush of eight tufts and sent for it, too; the eight-tufts toothbrush would amply demonstrate the martyr's frugality before his death. Unfortunately, during the life-and-death forward march, Liang Sanxi had cast off both his mug and toothbrush somewhere on foreign soil.

We searched for whatever photos Liang Sanxi might have left, but couldn't find any. Finally, from the biographical files that the divisional personnel department kept on the officers, we were able to obtain a two-inch-square photo of Liang Sanxi. It was the only likeness the artist had to go on when he painted Liang Sanxi's portrait.

I was disgusted with myself! I used to be a photographer in the corps' publicity department and had my own Yashika when I got to Company Nine, but I never took a picture of Liang Sanxi.

We were also left empty-handed after searching for any of his letters home or other written words of bravery. He had finished his second year of high school when he joined the army, so he ought to have been able to leave a few glorious words behind. The only thing we found were the notes that he had prepared in a notebook for drill instruction, all written in military terminology and hardly revealing the lofty thoughts of a martyr. In fact, the only thing he had held onto in his rush across the battlefield was the blood-stained list of his debts. When I showed the list of debts to the cadres in the regiment political department, they said that this kind of thing is not rare at all. Of the officers of platoon and company rank who had died in the battle, many were in debt. Company Five lost four officers and three of them were in debt. These debtors were without exception from the countryside. The amount of indebtedness varied from one man to another; Liang Sanxi was at the top of the list. It was not until then that I realized how unaware I had been of those rural officers and soldiers, unaware of their happiness and their sadness.

A few more days passed and Liang Sanxi's mother and wife were still nowhere to be seen. I insisted several times that the regiment political department make inquiries about them. The political department called me back one day to say that they had made a few calls to the civil administration department of Shandong Province and finally found out that Liang's mother, Aunt Liang, and his wife, Han Yuxiu, who was caring for a 3-month-old baby, had been on their way for more than ten days.

More than ten days? By bus . . . then train . . . then by bus again . . . . I counted on my fingers the number of days the trip might take. The three generations should have arrived much earlier. Had they been in an accident? That would be too . . . .

I began to regret my thoughtlessness. What I should have done was suggest to the regiment political department that someone be sent to Yimeng, Shandong, to bring the three generations here. The bus stop was not far from our company camp. For several days I sent soldiers there to meet the travelers, but the men came back empty-handed. I became more and more worried.

One day at noon, the division's jeep drove into the company camp. I saw my mother get out.

I led her into my dormitory and poured her a cup of water. "Ma . . . you have just arrived here today?" I didn't know what to say.

"Well, I traveled part of the way by plane, then the rest of the way by train. The division's jeep came to pick me up at the station. I stayed at the division for a while. So, now, here I am."

We lapsed into silence, looking at each other. Mother appeared even more emaciated than last time I saw her, on my furlough before coming to Company Nine. The habitually elated look had disappeared from her face. Now there were pale rings around her eyes.

"You . . . why didn't you write to me?" she asked.

"I was too busy after we got back from Vietnam."

"You . . . you don't know how I suffered day after day!" Mother said with tearful eyes. "I didn't even know until I saw it in the newspaper . . . about Company Nine . . . that you had not been . . . ."

I had nothing to say in reply.

"That very evening I made a telephone call to the front. I waited for more than three hours before I got through to Thunder God. But what a . . . a tongue-lashing I got! Since then, I have had nightmares every night. Once, I dreamed of Thunder God pointing a pistol at you and ordering you to blow up a blockhouse. Another time, I dreamed I saw you with blood all over your face, and you were calling for me." Mother shed her tears. "I know that it was inappropriate for me to call at that time, but, Thunder God, he . . . he was absolutely ruthless! I am approaching sixty and I've been no coward. But you are my only son. I would rather I die instead of you." She began sobbing again.

What could I say to her? I had no right to blame my dear mother.

Mother was born in northern Anhui Province to a family living in abject poverty. When she was eight, she was sold into slavery to a landlord. In 1938, when the Japanese invaders were attempting to move south, the Kuomintang government blew up the dam at Huayuankou on the Yellow River, which resulted in the calamitous inundation of eastern Henan and northern Anhui. The roaring flood drowned Grandfather's entire family. Mother, who was sixteen at the time, survived the disaster by clinging to a large wooden washbasin in the landlord's house. In autumn that year, she wandered to the Yimeng Mountains, where she joined the revolution. She had been a nurse and a head nurse in the regimental medical unit, then instructor in the underground hospital, chief of the divisional health section . . . . She followed the army to fight in the Jinan Campaign and the Huaihai Campaign and then went south with the army. Mother served in more than one hundred battles. She pinned the medals that she won to a handkerchief, finally covering it completely, a testament to her glorious career. Her thrilling and legendary experiences in wartime could fill a book thicker than a brick.

And I took part in only one battle.

The hot, dry weather seemed unbearable. I took off my cap.

"Dear me! What happened?" She had seen the fresh scar on my forehead. "Was it a bullet wound?"

"No. Only a scratch—shrapnel from hand grenades."

"My God! Nearly . . . very nearly hit in the . . . . " Mother said in a trembling voice. "Pain? . . . Do you feel any pain?"

I shook my head.

I was becoming upset from watching Mother wipe at her tears.

She loved me, had spoiled me and doted upon me so much that she still regarded me as a little boy. I used to be so proud of her. I had felt so happy, so special to have such a mother. But now, everything she did—her talk, her behavior—made me uncomfortable. Even the Swiss Omega watch and its glittering band around her wrist, which had seemed so pleasant to the eye, was now disagreeable.

"Mengsheng, I will no longer implore this one or that one to transfer you to our military region." Mother wiped away more tears. "You shed your blood for our homeland, and now you have a clear conscience. The border area still has not been pacified. Why don't you put away the military uniform and get transferred to civilian work?"

I shook my head.

Mother stared at me in surprise. "What . . . . You?"

I didn't know how to reply to Mother. My only thought was this: maternal love is both holy and selfish.

Eleven

The next evening as I was having dinner with Mother, Duan Yuguo rushed into the room. "Hurry, Instructor! Commander's family has arrived."

I laid down my chopsticks and followed him to the room where we had received the families of the martyrs. Soldiers were already there, coming and going and busying themselves to help out. When I came in, Aunt Liang and Han Yuxiu saw me and stood up. The three-month-old baby girl was lying on the bed next to them.

Duan Yuguo said to Aunt Liang, "Auntie, this is our instructor." The old woman nodded to me. "Yes, yes. Thank you for all your trouble."

Aunt Liang looked not quite seventy. Her clothes, made of hand-woven cloth, had been patched in places. She was tall and stoop-shouldered, her hair gray and white. Her face was thin and bony. Her forehead, eyes, and nose were all lined with webs of wrinkles. She seemed to be suffering from eye disease—her sagging eyes were red in the corners—yet they gleamed with tenderness, feebleness, and a touch of absent-mindedness, as though some bitter memories lay buried deep in them. How could I have believed that this was the mother of Company Commander if I had met her out in the street?

I went up to her and took hold of her with both of my hands. "Auntie, please sit down."

I helped Aunt Liang sit down on the edge of the bed, then turned to Han Yuxiu. "Xiao Han, please take a seat."

As soon as Yuxiu sat down, the baby woke up and started to cry. Yuxiu turned away to nurse the baby, and softly soothed her, who knew nothing at all. "Panpan, good girl, never cry, never cry . . . . "

"Auntie, I heard you started traveling more than ten days ago. What took you so long to get here?"

Before I could finish, Duan Yuguo whispered in my ear that they had traveled on foot all the way from the railway station.

"What?" I shuddered. It was more than 160 li from the railway station to the company camp. How did the three generations manage to climb over the mountains all by themselves? It was not until then that I noticed their shoes and trouser legs were covered with the red mud of the south. There had been a rain the previous day, and what a mess the road must have been!

Duan Yuguo said to Aunt Liang, "Auntie, there is a bus stop not far from the railway station and the bus can drive you right to the foot of the mountain. Didn't you hear about using the long-distance bus stop?"

Yuxiu answered in a low voice, "Yes, we heard."

Aunt Liang added, "It doesn't matter if us country women walk."

"How many days did you walk?" asked Duan Yuguo.

"Four and a half days," answered Yuxiu, still nursing the baby. "We might have gotten here faster if we hadn't had to ask directions along the way." I winked at Duan to stop him from asking any more questions.

The regiment had sent enough money for traveling expenses when they invited the family members of each of the martyrs to come to the unit. Had these people come here on foot to save a few yuan, or to spend the money on something else? The debt of 620 yuan that Liang Sanxi had left did explain the hardship of his family life.

The kitchen police leader came in with a few soldiers carrying four cooked dishes and a pot of hot noodles. They filled bowls with the noodles and asked Aunt Liang and Yuxiu to have dinner at the table.

Aunt Liang picked up a knapsack from the bed. It was made of mosquito netting cloth and had gotten soiled during their travel to the unit. She opened the nearly empty bag. I could see some dark pieces of pancake and salted radishes. Aunt Liang gathered the small pieces and put them into the noodle bowl.

The kitchen police leader walked over to stop her. "Auntie, don't eat those leftover crumbs."

"We didn't eat it all up on the way. It's okay to have them with noodle soup. It'd break my heart to throw them away, my child." She went on dropping crumbs into her bowl.

My eyes moistened with tears. Not until this moment did I understand why Liang Sanxi had gotten so angry when I threw away a loaf of steamed bread.

After eating, Aunt Liang and Yuxiu lay down to rest. I went back to company headquarters and called up the regiment political department to inform them of the arrival of Liang Sanxi's family. Secretary Gao, who answered the phone, told me that the political department had written letters to Aunt Liang and Han Yuxiu twice, asking them to bring photos of Liang Sanxi and the letters that he had written home. Secretary Gao told me to ask Aunt Liang and Yuxiu for the photos and letters so that the items representing Martyr Liang Sanxi in the Heroic Deeds Exhibition would not be too scant. Both the corps and divisional political departments had called to urge that Gao see to this matter.

The next day, after breakfast, I went to see Aunt Liang and Yuxiu again. Several squad and platoon leaders had already been to the room. Yuxiu had visited the company in March of last year and become acquainted with many of the men.

Yuxiu looked quite young, average in height with a well-proportioned figure. Her face, just as Jin Kailai had said, bore a strong resemblance to Tao Yuling, who played Chunni in *The Guards under Neon Lights*. Her beautiful long eyes and brows, and her delicate skin, too—were it not for mourning and tear stains on her face—would impress anybody with its special tenderness and tranquility. She was wearing a bluish white blouse with black trousers, both parts bordered in white thread. Two strips of white cloth were stuck to both shoes. I later learned that she was following the ancient Yimeng customs of mourning for her husband.

Seeing me come in, she stood up and nodded to me, a faint smile flickering across her face. But the smile was as brief as the flower that blooms in the storm: it is wilted in a flash, leaving only a sentimental memory for busy passers-by.

The soldiers were all smoking silently, and I could see that not one of them could think of anything to talk about with the old mother and widow. I had warned the whole company the night before that anyone who let the family know about Liang Sanxi's debts, purposely or unwittingly, would be strictly disciplined. The soldiers accepted this decree of mine with tears in their eyes.

Now I had to consider how to start. Perhaps first I should bring up Company Commander's heroic deeds on the battlefield to Aunt Liang and Yuxiu; then I could ask about the photos and letters. But when I saw the three-month-old baby girl and Yuxiu, who quietly hung her head, my heart began to ache with guilt.

If it had not been for my "curvilinear transfer," the superiors would have sent someone else to be the instructor of Company Nine. Then, Liang Sanxi would have been able to take his furlough in time and see his wife for the last time before he died on the battlefield. What's more, it was for my sake that he was . . . .

"Xiu, those comrades wrote us for the pictures or something," said Aunt Liang. "So, come on. Find them for us."

Yuxiu stood up and brought out a bundle wrapped in blue and white cloth. She took out half of an old envelope and handed it to me. "Instructor, he left no other pictures besides these two. One was taken when he was five years old. The other one was taken after he joined the army."

I took the half envelope from her and pulled out the two-inch photo. It was printed from the same negative as the one in the divisional personnel department.

When I took out the second faded yellow photo, I was stupefied. In the picture there was a country woman aged 35 or 36, with pitch-dark hair rolled in a bun. She looked healthy and sturdy, cracking a kind smile. Two boys of about the same age snuggled up in her arms. The headline at the top of the photo read

'Big Cat' and 'Little Cat' with Mother
May, 1952, Shanghai

I let out a cry of astonishment, as if I had been jolted with electricity. I myself had the same photo, which I kept in the album that I had used as a school boy.

I felt my head buzzing. I turned to Aunt Liang. "Auntie, this photo . . . . "

Auntie leaned toward me and pointed to the photo. "This is Big Cat, my boy Sanxi. This is Little Cat, the child of a military man. They took this picture the year I went to Shanghai to take Little Cat to his parents."

I felt suddenly dizzy, as if my whole body were adrift upon a cloud. Oh! God of destiny, how many partings and reunions you have arranged!

When I was a teenager, Mother had told me the story many times. The Kuomintang had waged a vigorous offensive against liberated areas around Yimeng Mountain, in Shandong. After the Menglianggu Campaign, the main force of our army made a sally out of the territory we held in order to destroy the enemy's offensive.

I was born at that time. Mother came down with malaria three days after my birth and had no milk for me. I cried with hunger. The local government sent Mother and me to a village at the foot of Meng Mountain. There was a woman Communist cadre in the village who was also a model partisan in supporting the resistance effort. Her own baby had been born ten days before I was. The woman nursed the two babies with both breasts. To protect me from the landlords' hired thugs, she said that her baby and I were twins. She named her own son Big Cat, and me, Little Cat.

Mother also told me that the woman cadre had been very kind to us. She always nursed me first and left Big Cat crying from hunger. Mother stayed in her home for one month while recovering from malaria. Then she went down south with the army.

The woman cadre took me back to my parents in Shanghai before I was quite five years old. When she quietly left with Big Cat, I flew into a tearful fit that went on for more than ten days, crying out for Ma and brother Big Cat.

"Instructor, you . . . . "
"Instructor, what's wrong with you?"
In a daze I heard my comrades calling me.
"Auntie!" I cried out and threw myself into Aunt Liang's arms.
Aunt Liang gently pushed me back. "What's the matter, my child?"
"Auntie, I . . . I was that Little Cat!"

"What?" Aunt Liang loosened her grasp on me and rubbed the corners of her red eyes. She gazed at me and then shook her head. "No, it's . . . impossible."

"Yes, Auntie. I really am Little Cat!" I cried.

"You are . . . the son of Commander Zhao?"

"Yes. He was the corps commander when our army troops attacked Menglianggu."

"Your mother is Wu. Wu—"

"Yes, Wu Shuang."

Aunt Liang remained speechless for a while. When I again threw myself to her knees, she stroked my head and murmured, "A dream, is it a dream?"

Nestled once again in Aunt Liang's arms, I was in turmoil. Aunt Liang was my mother who had brought me up; Liang Sanxi, my brother Big Cat. How could we be divided into superior and inferior? We had both been brought up on the milk of the same mother. We were of the same root.

Twelve

You can imagine how shaken I was by this reunion.

When I showed the faded picture to Mother, she was stupefied, too. She asked me to take her to the room where Aunt Liang was staying.

Aunt Liang stood up slowly. They looked at each other for a moment. Obviously, neither one recognized the other.

For the first few years after Aunt Liang sent me to my parents in May, 1952, our families stayed in touch by mail. Mother never forgot to send some money to Aunt Liang's family for New Year's Day and other festivals. Aunt Liang would send us seasonal treats from Shandong—walnuts, dates, and peanuts. But Mother's correspondence grew less frequent year after year. When the Cultural Revolution started, friendships and relationships succumbed to the prevailing winds. The two families slipped out of touch and had had no contact since then.

"Sister Liang, you . . . . " Mother, who had always had a talent for diplomacy, was now tongue-tied.

"Lao Wu, is that you indeed, Lao Wu?" Aunt Liang's wrinkled face split into a smile. "You called me 'Sister Liang' then, and you let me call you Sister Shuang, didn't you?"

"Yes," Mother answered.

"Lao Wu!" Aunt Liang took a step forward and touched my mother's arms with her bark-rough hands. "It was not easy for you to live safely through the turmoil. That no-good gang of flatterers—those goddamn, evil flatterers! You must have had such a hard time."

Mother couldn't find the words to answer.

Aunt Liang's gaze passed over my mother. "It's been almost thirty years since the last time we saw each other. Hmmm, you don't look too old; you sure don't. How is Commander Zhao?" She still addressed my father by his old title.

"He's fine," Mother said, nodding. Any other time she would have spouted a flood of words about the persecution my father had suffered.

"We'll rest easy as long as you and Lao Zhao are all right." Aunt Liang heaved a sigh. "At the start of the turmoil, someone came to me to find out if you and Lao Zhao had ever turned traitor before the Liberation. Well, you should have seen the look I gave him! Us Yimeng Mountain folk may not be fancy speakers, but we won't go against our conscience. Everybody in our area knew you and Commander Zhao. You were such fine people. How much of your own blood you have shed for our people's state power!" Aunt Liang lifted the edge of her coat to wipe away her tears.

"Sister Liang, you . . . . Please sit down." Mother helped Aunt Liang into a chair. Yuxiu and I took our seats, too. I could read the distress on Mother's face. The less Aunt Liang complained, the more disturbed Mother and I felt.

Mother gazed at Aunt Liang. "Sister Liang, your whole *family* . . . ."

"Here . . . here we are, my whole family," said Aunt Liang quietly. "This is my daughter-in-law, Yuxiu. The baby sleeping there is my granddaughter, Panpan."

Silence.

"Oh." Aunt Liang heaved a deep sigh, and said to Mother, "You knew about my eldest son. His nickname was 'Tiedan'—'Iron Ball.' He got his formal name, Daxi, when he became head of the Children's Corps. Daxi had been a partisan messenger for the Eighth Route Army when he was eight years old. Those traitors to China captured him when he was twelve . . . ." Aunt Liang stopped.

I remembered the story Mother told me about Tiedan. He had been a messenger from the time he was eight years old, and had delivered almost a hundred letters without making any mistakes. The older messengers and the officers of the Eighth Route Army often praised him for his shrewdness. But he was finally caught by some traitors while delivering a message. He quickly wadded the note and then chewed it up. The Japanese soldiers tried to force him to talk, and the traitors broke off all of his teeth with a hammer, but he wouldn't say a word. Then a Japanese soldier pressed a bayonet flat against his nose and threatened to kill him. Tiedan still wouldn't yield, and the Japanese soldier stabbed him to death.

After a long while, Mother asked, "Sister Liang, you have a son two years older than Mengsheng, don't you? His name is—"

"Oh, you mean Erxi." Aunt Liang turned to Yuxiu. "Xiu, in which year did Erxi die?"

"During the turmoil, 1967, the year against the 'Adverse Current.' He . . . . "

"Yes, that summer. The senior cadres were either criticized or taken into custody. With the help of villagers, many hid themselves up on Maling Mountain. Before long, an armed gang followed them to the mountain and set up a siege. Then the fighting started. They used hand grenades, machine guns, even cannon. Erxi had led the county magistrate into the mountain and then was killed by a cannon. I heard afterward that one shell killed more than ten villagers. They were all buried right where they died. I never found out where Erxi was buried . . . . But, please, don't bring it up again. It's all over and done with."

Maybe she had cried all her tears many years ago; it had been more than ten years since Erxi's tragic death. The old woman had talked in a soft voice, as if she were telling a story from the *Arabian Nights*, rather than recounting a family tragedy.

Mother wiped her tears with a handkerchief. Then she said in a trembling voice, "And Brother Liang, was he also . . . in the turmoil? . . . "

"You mean Sanxi's father. It was the year of killing the date trees . . . . "

Yuxiu interrupted her mother-in-law. "It was the year of criticizing Lin Biao and Confucius, not killing the date trees."

"Whatever name it was called, it was that spring, when Sanxi's father got distension of the abdomen." Aunt Liang turned to my mother. "Lao Wu, you know why our village is called Date Blossom Valley. We used to have lots of date trees. On the hill south of the village alone there used to be more than two thousand three hundred date trees. When the trees came into bloom, even our breath smelled sweet. The date groves used to be the lifeblood of our villagers. By selling dates, the wives could get money to buy cooking oil and salt. The young women and girls would buy printed cloth.

"Lao Wu—you knew Sanxi's father. He had tried to deliver some grain for our troops during the Huaihai Campaign, but got wounded in the leg by shrapnel from Chiang Kai-shek's army. Well, because of that, he couldn't do heavy farm work when they set up the agricultural cooperative, so he was assigned to watch the date woods on the hill south of the village.

"In that year of killing the date trees, a work team was sent to our village and we were forced to cut down all the date trees to make the land into 'Dazhai' terraces. When he saw that they were cutting the date trees down one by one, my husband broke down, just bawling. The oldest date tree of them all stood at the top of the hill. It had been spared when the Kuomintang soldiers cut down the trees to build their defense works. Our villagers called it 'Old Man Tree.' My husband held onto Old Man Tree and said that he would rather be cut down with the tree. But he was sent rolling by a hard kick . . . and he never stood up again . . . .

"Our neighbors brought him home on a door plank. His belly got bloated real bad and stayed that way from then on. He just laid in bed, puffing and blowing.

"The next summer, after everyone in the village—young and old—had worked on the terraces, a heavy storm came and washed away all the topsoil into the Yi River. After that, not even grass would grow on the hill, let alone new date trees.

"Nobody in the village dared to tell Sanxi's father, who still laid there puffing and blowing on the bed. For more than two years he laid there. He was such a burden to Sanxi, who had already joined the army by then. Sanxi was bent on getting his father cured and sent money time and again for us to buy medicine. Yuxiu and Sanxi hadn't gotten married yet, but she was the one who came over to help us. Medicinal herbs and tablets . . . she was the only one who kept track of how many herbs had been stewed so he could drink the juice. Later on, when money aplenty had been spent, Sanxi's father breathed his last."

Finally, I understood why Liang Sanxi had left the blood-stained list of 620 yuan in debts.

After a while, Aunt Liang said to Mother, "Sanxi's father had talked about Commander Zhao on his deathbed. He said, 'If only Commander Zhao were here. With his short temper, he would have had them eating bullets!'"

Neither Mother nor I answered. Even if Father had been present, what could he have done? There was no doubt in my mind that in those years Father had often talked and behaved against his own conscience. He had 'drawn in his horns amidst the fierce storm,' as they say. Warriors like Commander Lei who dared to "slam his cap" a few times were pretty rare after all.

"Lao Wu, I shouldn't have brought up those old cares from the past. They'll only grieve you." Aunt Liang again took a long look at my mother. "It's all over with, now. They say Chairman Mao left his last instructions to catch that gang of flatterers. Now, thanks to him, all of those flatterers have been caught one by one by our Party. Now us peasants are starting to feel hopeful again. Hopeful!"

Panpan woke up on her bed and started to cry.

Yuxiu got up, held Panpan in her arms and nursed her, but the baby went on crying.

Mother stood up. "What's the matter? Is she sick?"

"No, she isn't," said Yuxiu, rocking the baby in her arms. "Good girl, don't cry, never cry . . . . "

Aunt Liang said, "It's the shortage of milk. Yuxiu learned the news about Sanxi one month after the child was born. Since then, she hasn't had enough milk to nurse the baby."

After the encounter with Aunt Liang and her family, and seeing for herself Liang Sanxi's blood-stained list of debts, my mother felt so bad that she shed many tears. She never mentioned my transfer to civilian work again.

Mother and I began to discuss how we could help Aunt Liang and her family. Mother hadn't brought much money with her, and I hadn't kept a very large account here either because I had been expecting a transfer.

The next afternoon, when the kitchen police leader was about to go into town for provisions, I asked him to sell my Yashika at the commission shop and to borrow 1,000 yuan from the Regimental Logistics Department. I told him that it was an emergency.

Mother repeatedly exhorted the kitchen police leader, "Don't forget. Buy ten packs of milk powder, four bottles of orange juice, a milk pot, and a feeding bottle."

The new cemetery of martyrs was situated halfway up Company Nine's mountain. The third morning after Aunt Liang's family arrived, we accompanied the three generations to Liang Sanxi's grave. Like the family members of all the other martyrs, mother and daughter-in-law stood silently before the grave for a while without shedding a tear. The only difference was that Aunt Liang and Yuxiu, carrying the baby in her arms, walked around the grave seven times from the left and seven times from the right. I learned later that it was an old funeral custom in the Yimeng Mountains.

Two days later, the kitchen police leader came back. He gave me the 1,000 yuan borrowed from the Regimental Logistics Department, and the milk powder. I put aside 620 yuan to pay off Liang Sanxi's debts, and, with the money I had on hand, got together another 500 yuan for Aunt Liang.

Once again Mother and I entered Aunt Liang's room.

Mother opened a pack of milk powder and explained to Yuxiu how to mix the right amounts of powder and water. Then she put a measure of the powder into the milk-pot and began to mix the powder with water. When the milk was ready she poured it into the bottle, checked the temperature, then picked up the baby in her arms to feed her.

Panpan sucked the milk hungrily.

Aunt Liang stood smiling beside them. "When I heard from the young people of our village that there was such a thing as this in town, I couldn't believe it. Well, it's just wonderful. People are so smart. The man-made nipple is just like the real one. It's really wonderful!"

Panpan soon had enough. Mother laid her on the bed. She looked around with her bright black eyes, her little mouth cracking a sweet smile.

Aunt Liang was even more pleased. She turned to Yuxiu. "Xiu, now you don't have to worry . . . nothing to worry about."

The more excited Aunt Liang looked, the more my heart ached. How faraway they had been from modern civilization.

I took out the 500 yuan and put it in front of Aunt Liang. "Auntie, please accept the money."

"Oh, no . . . . No, my child, I can't." Aunt Liang took up the money with her bark-like hands. "I can't take that." She insisted on tucking the money back into my pocket. Three times I took the money out of my pocket but Aunt Liang persistently returned it to me three times.

"Sister Liang," said Mother sadly; "If we . . . haven't offended you, then please . . . accept the money!"

"Oh, don't say that, Lao Wu," said Aunt Liang. "You bought so much milk powder for Panpan. It's been a great help to us. I really can't spend any more of your money. Life is easy in the countryside. I have some money of my own, anyway. It's no problem."

Before Mother and I left the room, I put the 500 yuan on the bed.

Yuxiu rushed out of the room. "Instructor, no . . . please don't. My mother-in-law can't take this money, and neither can I. Come on, take it back. Really, I have my own money."

I went back to my room feeling dejected.

Mother muttered to herself, "Those mountaineers—that's the way those people are."

Oh, mountaineers! Didn't we all come from some remote mountain area? I had been a follower of materialism the past few years, but what had just happened made me realize that there are, after all, things that are more precious than money and power in this world, things that are worth cherishing and pursuing. I had felt some relief after I thought I'd found a way to pay off Liang Sanxi's 620-yuan debt, but this relief soon gave way to a stronger feeling of remorse. Even if I had the means to pay off his debts secretly, the debt of gratitude that Mother and I owed the Yimeng people could never be repaid with money or jewels.

Thirteen

One afternoon, Secretary Gao arrived at Company Nine by bike. Before he had laid aside his bicycle, he was telling me excitedly, "There is important news we can report . . . important news!"

I couldn't imagine why he was so excited.

"They've located Soldier Beijing's family."

"Where?" I asked. "Has anyone from his family arrived here?"

"Take a guess. Your heroic soldier, 'Beijing'—or Xue Kaihua . . . ." Secretary Gao gazed at me cryptically. "Do you know who his father is?"

I shook my head.

"Commander Lei! Xue Kaihua is Commander Lei's son!"

"Oh!" I was bewildered. A moment later, I asked, still puzzled, "Then why was his surname Xue?"

"Because Commander's wife's family name is Xue. Kaihua took his mother's family name," said Secretary Gao talking nonstop. "I learned from a clerk at the corps headquarters that our corps commander has four daughters. The only son was Xue Kaihua. The eldest daughter is surnamed Xue but the other three took the name Lei. The eldest daughter took her mother's family name 'Xue' because, during the war, the Kuomintang had committed several massacres in Commander's wife's hometown, and it would be very difficult for a Red Army soldier's child to avoid getting butchered, too. As for Kaihua, I heard he got the name because of Commander's strict sense of discipline. When the boy started school, the father had to enroll him under a family name. Commander asked him whether he liked his father or mother best, and the boy firmly answered 'Mother.' Commander burst into laughter and said, 'All right. You can take your mother's family name.' So he named his son Xue Kaihua." Secretary Gao stopped the story abruptly and asked me, "Well, Commander Lei has come by your company. Haven't you seen him?"

"No."

"Isn't that strange?" Secretary Gao stood speechless for a moment, then said, "Commander first came to our regiment in a jeep. He said he was leaving for Company Nine, and I rode as fast as I could to follow his jeep here."

Hearing this, I walked out of the room with Secretary Gao. We looked around the whole barracks, but neither the corps commander nor his jeep was in sight.

We went back to the company headquarters. Secretary Gao took a moment to dip a towel in some water and wiped the sweat from his face.

"I heard that Commander found out about Kaihua's death a long time ago, but he is still keeping the news from his wife." After a pause, Secretary Gao continued, "Comrade Kaihua had left a letter, which was found in his breast pocket before the divisional collecting team buried him. Since he had signed it only as 'Kaihua,' nobody associated the name with the corps commander at first. Commander Lei has the original letter now. But I have a mimeographed copy that was made by the divisional publicity section." Secretary Gao opened his small briefcase and handed me the letter. "Here. Read it. This letter has a very deep significance, because it shows that the author had some remarkable talents."

I took the letter and began to read in earnest.

Dear Papa,

I came all the way to the front from Beijing Command in such a hurry that I was able to meet with you only once. I kept it short because I knew that on the eve of the battle, time would be very precious for you.

I took your advice and came to Company Nine, which is to be the point company in this battle. It's still a big question mark for both of us as to how fierce a battle this is going to be for Company Nine.

Last winter, after you had read both of my 1,000-word articles in Military Science magazine, you wrote to me with so much encouragement, telling me that I had the makings of a general. To tell you the truth, dear Papa, your Kaihua wants not only to be a general, he wants to be a marshal as well!

"Oh, My twenty-one-year-old Kaihua talks with such bold sentences!"
you may be thinking. Is it ambition? Aspiration? Well, it doesn't matter. I
have the greatest esteem for Napoleon's idea that "The soldier who doesn't
want to be a general will not be a good soldier." Of course, not all soldiers
get to be generals. But look at the world picture: today's dazzling,
materialistic civilization poses such an irresistible attraction to my generation. But my belief is this: there is no cradle in the flower garden for a future
general, and indulging in tender love does not develop the qualities of a
general. A soldier who sticks to the big city of Beijing will never turn himself
into a marshal! A marshal must be of those soldiers who truly understand
what it means to be a soldier, who have fought the battlefield's life-and-death
struggles. Because I think this way, I have requested to be transferred out
of the capital and to the front in order to fulfill my "dream of the future
marshal."

Dear Papa, I've read most of the foreign military books that you
recommended to me last year. In your fifty-seventh year you are still
devoting yourself to the study of foreign military strategies. How I admire
you! I remember that you once wrote in a letter, "A mere warrior will no
longer be able to handle wars in the future." I was particularly inspired by
the fact that the words came from you, Father. Those who consider soldiers
to be the simplest of souls have made a mistake—a big mistake! In the old
days, "millet plus rifle" may have worked against the Japanese invaders but
those days are gone, never to return—not to mention using spears or swords
as weapons. Modern science and technology progress with each passing
day, and the powerful countries of the world all apply their most advanced
scientific technology to producing military armaments. The small earth
travels forty thousand kilometers every single day—how amazing the speed!
And how many new problems does fighting a modern war pose to our
marshals and soldiers! How dangerous it will be if our feet tread up the ramp
of a Boeing 747 but our brains still rest on horseback. The Confucianists
have met with a good deal of misfortune over the past few years, but I still
hope each of our generals and marshals can attain both the gallant manner
of a warrior and the literary grace of a Confucianist.

On writing this, dear Papa, I feel a pity for our elder generation. You
were in middle age when the gun salute for the founding of the People's
Republic of China was fired. Suppose that since that glorious day your
generation had scaled the heights of military science with the same
determination that you used against the enemy's blockhouses—what a
grand accomplishment that would be! But on the contrary, one political

movement after another—the whirlpool of the great storms—drained away your best days and, along with them, so many of the material and spiritual values of the Chinese nation. What is worse, some people used the turmoil as an opportunity to abuse their power in the pursuit of personal gain, which made the situation all the more lamentable.

I understand, Papa, that there is no use in complaining about our yesterday. Let you of the elder generation lead us of the younger to the rescue of our tomorrow!

Dear Papa, the troops are going to be mustered soon. As a serviceman who has spent over half his life in the military, you well know what it means to go to war. If I as a soldier sacrifice my life on the battlefield, I won't, of course, have the whole nation attending my funeral—"the future marshal"—but with my head resting on the lofty mountain of my motherland and my body buried in the red soil of the southern border, I'll take no pity on my death, nor shall I feel any qualms as a son of China.

It's a cinch that we shall win the battle. The day of victory is not far off.

I wish Papa the best of health.

Lovingly yours,
Kaihua
4 p.m., Feb. 16, 1979

Papa, our jiaozi is not ready yet. Let me add a few more sentences: if I die in the battle, please conceal the news from my dearest mother as long as possible. If I know that your strict, fatherly love kept me from being reduced to a playboy, then I also know that Mother's sincere affection for her son let me feel the warmth of this world. Even now, as I think of Mother, my tears spill onto the paper. During Father's misfortune, it was Mother who guided me past the perilous crossroads of life. Her heart is not too strong and would not bear a severe shock.

Mother has often urged me to adopt my Father's surname. Once I am dead, I would like to follow Mother's wishes. Please report it as such to my superior.

P.S. When Father stands in front of my grave, I hope you won't take off your cap. Your son would be happy for you to have a look at my resting place. But I associate your taking off the cap with your slamming it down.

Each time you did so, it brought you bad luck. Although I want you to carry on your "cap slamming" spirit, I am also afraid that the days that made you follow through may come again. I'm probably worrying about nothing because history and the one billion population won't allow that kind of tragedy to brew again.

Yours,
Kaihua

I was greatly touched by the letter.

"Instructor Zhao, you . . . . " Seeing that I was shedding tears, Secretary Gao was puzzled.

I hadn't thought I was too sentimental a person. But as a man who had witnessed Kaihua's wisdom and courage, this letter upset me in a way that would not affect someone else.

Outside the house we heard the sound of a jeep. Secretary Gao and I went out and saw Commander Lei's jeep, but Commander himself wasn't in it. The driver told us that Commander had come all the way from regiment headquarters to battalion. He was now in the cemetery of the martyrs and would come to company headquarters soon.

Secretary Gao and I trotted along the road to the new cemetery of martyrs that had just been constructed halfway up the mountain. We found Commander Lei standing in front of a tombstone inscribed with the words "Grave of Martyr Xue Kaihua," silently mourning the death of the martyr. Probably in accordance with his son's wish, Lei hadn't taken off his cap. After a moment, he took a step backward, solemnly raised his right hand, and saluted his dead son. A good while later, he lowered his right hand slowly.

Secretary Gao and I quietly went up to him. We saw Commander Lei weeping. Tears streamed down his old face and dripped onto his chest.

"Following Kaihua's last wish, will you please instruct the regiment political department to . . . have Kaihua's surname changed," Commander said to me in a hoarse voice. "Would you also replace the tombstone, changing 'Xue' into 'Lei'?"

I wiped my tearful eyes and nodded assent.

Secretary Gao opened his camera, preparing to take a picture as a keepsake for Commander in front of his son's tombstone, but Commander signaled to him not to do it.

"Are you the one who writes the regiment's news reports?"

"Yes," answered Secretary Gao, standing at attention.

"The propaganda on Kaihua must be done according to the facts."

"Yes."

"Don't make an issue of Kaihua's changing his surname. Still call him Xue Kaihua in the report."

"Yes."

"Kaihua is Kaihua. My name mustn't appear in the article. You will not heap praises on me under the pretext of praising Kaihua."

"Yes."

"Conduct an investigation into why Jin Kailai, who was vice-commander of Company Nine, didn't win a merit award."

"Yes."

"And send it to me in ten days."

"Yes."

"Jin Kailai was a good man on the battlefield."

"Yes."

"You go back first," said Commander Lei to Secretary Gao and me. "I'll stay here a while longer."

Secretary Gao and I turned to leave the cemetery of martyrs. After we had walked some ten steps or so, we looked back and saw Commander sitting on his heels, his head hanging low and one hand resting on the tombstone. He was shaking all over. As we turned away and walked down the mountain, we could hear Commander's faint sobs.

Fourteen

I told Mother about the relationship between Kaihua and Commander Lei. At first she was stunned; then she sighed, but made no other reply.

I left Mother's room and waited on the path outside of the barracks for Commander Lei, who came down from the hill after a while.

He called on Aunt Liang and her family before coming to the company headquarters. There, he sat down and inquired into the circumstances of Aunt Liang's family and their misfortunes, and examined Liang Sanxi's list of debts. He instructed me to find time to chat with Aunt Liang and Han Yuxiu, and that our company should do as much as possible to help Aunt Liang's family solve some of their most immediate problems. For things that would have to be dealt with over the long run, we were to report to the local government through our superior.

At dinner time, Commander himself went to invite Aunt Liang's family to company headquarters, and sat with them at dinner. Commander also told me to have Mother join the group, but she pleaded that she didn't feel well and stayed away.

After dinner, Commander asked me to lead him to Mother's room.

"Welcome, Sister Wu. Excuse me for not meeting you when you arrived," Commander Lei said as he stepped in. "Of course, I know you've been avoiding me."

Mother had been lying down on the bed, but she sat up and nodded to him.

He said, "I came to Company Nine to visit Kaihua's grave. But, above all, I want to see you—Sister Wu! I should make it clear from the start that I did not come here to offer you an apology." He sat down.

Mother, obviously embarrassed, made no reply.

"To tell you the truth, Sister Wu, I anticipated that you might try to get even with me after the battle, and I prepared myself for a lot of crying about your son." Commander lit up a cigarette and took a deep drag. "Yes, Mengsheng didn't die on the battlefield, but it was a very close call."

"Lao Lei, please don't . . . . "

"No. Let me finish my words. True, I cursed you over the telephone. My patience was exhausted. You could hate me, the 'Thunder God,' for contradicting the normal human impulse to help others, but I don't regret what I did. You were so bold, Sister Wu! You might have asked Zhao Mengsheng's father to deal with me: he could have *commanded* me to execute his orders. But I figured he wouldn't do that—and he didn't dare to! Did you . . . had you thought it over before you held up my forward command post's telephone line just to talk about your son's transfer?" Commander had become very agitated while he talked. His fingers heavily drummed the desk top. However, once he had suppressed his anger, Commander continued. "If the clock were turned back thirty years and I, Thunder God, asked you to violate the code of a soldier, what would you do? A dressing down or two slaps on the face would hardly even be punishment. I would have deserved it even if you'd given me a bullet. Remember how it was back then? That song, 'Wife sees husband off to the front/ Mother sends son to fight the Japanese'—you taught it to me, line by line, Sister Wu. My blood used to burn with outrage then!"

"No, Lao Lei, please don't . . . . " Mother began to sob.

"I must. I have a lot to say tonight. I want to tell you that this time I would like to oblige your request. Your Lao Lei didn't forget his words. A gentleman would go to any lengths to repay a debt of gratitude. If you, Sister Wu, had not carried me out of the heaps of corpses, would I, Thunder God, be alive today as the corps commander?" Commander stubbed out his cigarette and stood up. "All right. As long as Mengsheng himself agrees, you can take him back, either in uniform or out of uniform. I believe in being straightforward. I'll sign his orders for transfer.

"Lao Lei . . . " Mother cried.

"But after I have approved his transfer, I want you to examine your own conscience. Am I paying you back for saving my life? Am I pushing you into the mire of influence peddling? Would the martyrs agree with what you want? Would the people who had supported us agree? In the fall of 1942, only forty-three of the four hundred members of my battalion survived the battle by breaking out of the encirclement—including myself, who was carried away from the heaps of corpses by you, Sister Wu . . . . "

Commander's voice became hoarse. He drew out his handkerchief, wiped his moist eyes, and sat down again. He lit up another cigarette and exhaled the smoke softly.

Mother kept wiping her eyes. Glancing at her, Commander said in a milder tone, "We won state power through armed struggle and the shedding of our blood. We are ruling the country now. But arrogance and hedonism might destroy all that we have gained. After ten years of turmoil, the younger generation was scolded into seeing beyond worldly vanity; but what about our old guys? We do have some who don't think twice about using their power and influence for personal gain. As the saying goes, 'If the upper beam isn't positioned right, the lower ones will be crooked, too.' If we old people can't behave decently, how can we educate the younger generation? Mengsheng is a hero now and I won't scold him anymore. But think about it, Sister Wu: isn't it true that you were partly responsible for his past behavior?"

Mother nodded in tears.

Commander looked at Mother and said, "You were sold into slavery when you were eight. I grazed cattle for a landlord when I was seven. It may be pointless to talk to young people about our suffering in the past, but we old people still benefit from it. 'Forgetting the past means betrayal.' Lenin's words summed it up." Commander flicked his cigarette ashes and took another drag. "In 1965, when I attended a conference in Beijing, I had a long talk with Commander-in-Chief Chen Yi. Recalling the days when we were in Shandong, Commander Chen told me in a voice that was choked with emotion that he would never forget the people in Shandong as long as he was alive. He meant all our people! We should repay them to the end of our days for their sacrifices, instead of acting as their savior. It was with the people's millet that the revolution was raised. Because they pushed handcarts to transport our food and supplies, we won our victory."

The crescent moon had stretched its way into the window, casting its silver rays into the house. The room was completely quiet.

"I can't tell you how I felt when I saw Aunt Liang today," said Commander, full of emotion. "Sister Wu, your Mengsheng was brought up on Aunt Liang's milk. But—look at the clothes she was wearing and the debt lists Liang Sanxi left. You can see right away what kind of life they're living."

Commander's eyes glistened with tears. Mother was weeping, too.

"It is true that during the ten-year turmoil we old guys were persecuted. But it wasn't us who suffered most—it was the ordinary people like Aunt Liang. This is the truth: even when I was in custody, my food and clothes were better than the Liangs' . . . much better." Commander heaved a deep sigh. "My Kaihua, when he was fifteen, settled with his sister in the countryside of Mizhi County, in Yan'an. There, they lived with a peasant friend of mine, that I had lived with once. In the spring of 1977, before I resumed my post, I made a special trip to see my old friend in Mizhi County. You may not believe it, but they only had five bowls for the eight people in the family. They couldn't even afford to buy those black bowls. Seeing that, I . . . Yan'an was the sacred cradle of the revolution!"

"Oh, Lao Lei . . . please . . . please stop talking about it."

"All right, I'll stop. I'll have a good cry too, if I go on. The ordinary people time and again get 'bobtailed' when there is already hardly any meat left on their bones. But we have cars available whenever we want to go out, and we have fish for every meal. Leading such a comfortable life, would you ever bother your head about how well the ordinary folk were doing? We should examine our consciences. Our Communist Party made the revolution because there was poverty. It should have been our Party's mission to put an end to poverty."

The air in the room seemed to have coagulated. It oppressed me as heavily as a block of lead. I couldn't breathe.

I said to Commander in a low voice, "After the battle, many martyrs from our regiment left behind their debt lists. All of those men were from the countryside."

"I'll report it to the Central Committee," said Commander. "The ultra-leftist line did a great deal of harm to people."

After Commander had calmed himself down a few minutes later, he asked me about the last fight that Company Nine had taken part in. I gave him the details, laying much of the emphasis on Liang Sanxi and Jin Kailai's heroism in battle.

Commander stood up again. "These ordinary people: they didn't forget to concern themselves with the destiny of the country. Although the ten-year turmoil brought them endless misery, they still laid down their lives for the country when they were called!" Commander waved his right hand excitedly. "Our nation is great, and this is where the greatness shows. There is hope for our cause, and this is where the hope resides. Lu Xun wrote, 'The most precious thing is the nation's spirit.'" After a while, Commander sat down again and took a look at his watch. "It's not early—ten minutes to midnight."

He asked me about Kaihua's death. I answered without mentioning the dud shells. I couldn't bear having this valiant general slam his cap in anger once again.

The kitchen police leader pushed the door open and said to me in a flustered voice, "Instructor, Han Yuxiu's disappeared!"

I rushed out of the room. Seeing Aunt Liang in the courtyard, I asked her what had happened. She said that she had dozed off for a while, and when she turned on the lamp, Yuxiu was nowhere to be seen.

I was worried because we were so close to the border and Vietnamese spies infiltrated the area sometimes. All the soldiers quickly gathered round to help. We searched all around the barracks but didn't find her.

"Maybe she went to Sanxi's grave," Aunt Liang said to me. "Since she found out about Sanxi dying, she hasn't cried in front of me for fear she'd break my heart."

I hurriedly led some soldiers to the cemetery of the martyrs.

The crescent moon hung high in the sky. When we were about ten meters away from Liang Sanxi's grave, we saw a figure bending over it. It was Yuxiu, no doubt about that. I had my soldiers stop.

There, at the foot of the cliff, inside the stands of bamboo and weeds, we heard the thin chirping of insects but nothing of the sound of weeping.

After a long while, we crept up to Liang Sanxi's grave and found Yuxiu leaning over it, weeping silently. She was shivering all over.

"Xiao Han, you . . . go on and cry. Cry it all out," I whimpered. "That will make you feel better."

Hearing my voice, Yuxiu slowly got up. "No, Instructor, that's all right. I was only feeling a little . . . oppressed in the room . . . ." She wiped her tear-stained face with a sleeve. "It's nothing. I'm leaving with my mother-in-law, so I . . . I wanted to have a last look at the grave . . . ."

The stars twinkled all over the sky like so many eyes shedding tears. Everything below the firmament now blurred before me.

Fifteen

The next day, Commander Lei set off for military regional headquarters to attend a meeting. Before he left, he urged me once again to take good care of Aunt Liang and her family.

But after another week at the company headquarters, the two women began to talk about returning home. I knew I couldn't persuade them to stay any longer; besides, being at the company headquarters, near as it is to the fresh graves, would just continue their anguish. I thought it would be better to allow them leave now so that the system could work their problems out in its own way back in the village. The regimental superior agreed with me. Aunt Liang and her family were to leave Company Nine the next day, after breakfast.

The director of the regiment political department arrived at Company Nine in the afternoon to see the Liangs off, but also to determine what their specific problems were. For martyrs like Liang Sanxi, whose military rank didn't entitle him to bring his wife and child along with him, the consolation and compensation duties were usually coordinated between the troops and the local government. We also learned that there were stipulations attached to the compensation.

In the countryside, the parents of martyrs whose brothers were able-bodied farm workers might or might not be pensioned; the wife and each child could receive five to eight yuan each month, depending on the cost of living in their region. The regimental superior decided to report to the local government the fact that Aunt Liang had no one to depend on so she could receive special assistance from the local civil administration department.

Liang Sanxi left almost nothing to his family. When his two thread-bare uniforms were collected for the Heroic Deeds Exhibition, the regimental quartermaster issued two new replacement uniforms. Except for this, the only other item was the new uniform overcoat that Liang Sanxi had kept carefully wrapped in the big plastic bag.

I picked up the overcoat and the two new uniforms and took them over to Han Yuxiu to give them to her.

When the director of the regiment political department and I walked up to the building where Aunt Liang's room was located, we found Yuxiu outside washing some bed sheets and uniforms under the tap. In spite of resistance from the soldiers and me, Yuxiu had been keeping herself very busy. She helped the kitchen police wash the bread cloths and steam boxes. She unstitched, separated, and washed the soldiers' cotton-padded quilts.

"Xiao Han, stop washing," I said to Yuxiu. "Come inside with us. Director would like to talk to you and Auntie on behalf of the superior."

Yuxiu quietly stood up, dried her hands, and followed Director and me inside to Aunt Liang's room.

I laid the plastic bag with the uniforms and overcoat inside on Yuxiu's bed. "Xiao Han, this is what Commander Liang left behind." Just as her hands touched the plastic bag, she gave a scream and ran out of the room. I hurried after her.

"What's the matter with you, Xiao Han?"

Yuxiu's face was bathed in tears. She put her hands into the wash basin and forced herself to scrub the clothes on the washboard.

"Xiao Han . . . Director wants to talk to you."

She bit her lower lip and remained silent.

"Please let her wash, Mengsheng," called Aunt Liang from inside the building. "I told the comrades not to stop her from working. She's the kind that can't sit still. That would only make it more painful for her. Let her wash. Today could be the last day she ever washes for the comrades."

I saw in Yuxiu the traditional virtue of Chinese women. Still, I wondered why the uniform overcoat evoked such grief.

"Mengsheng, don't call her over. You can talk to me." Aunt Liang was speaking again.

Director and I sat down with Aunt Liang. He told her about the regimental superior's intentions.

Aunt Liang shook her head. "No, we don't have any problems."

We asked again, but Aunt Liang kept shaking her head. "No, really. We don't have any problems. We feel hopeful now. Life is easy out in the countryside."

Faced with such a sincere—and stubborn—old woman, Director and I had nothing else to say.

After a while, Aunt Liang, gazing at Director and me, did say, "There's only one thing I want you to do for me."

"Tell us, Auntie." Director opened his little notebook, ready to write down her request.

Aunt Liang heaved a sigh and said, "People think that our Liang ancestors must have burned many joss sticks to please the gods: we have such a nice daughter-in-law. Anyone can see she's good-looking. But she's good at needlework and all kinds of housework, too. As for farm work, there's hardly a thing she can't do very well. She is kind and gentle-natured. All the neighbors think I'm blest . . . . " Aunt Liang held up the front of her cloak to wipe her eyes. "But I feel so bad whenever I think about her. As a mother-in-law, I owe her so much. Before she and Sanxi got married, Sanxi's father had been sick for more than two years. I was hard up for money. When she did get married, I couldn't buy her anything, not . . . even a piece of cloth . . . . "

Aunt Liang was overcome with sorrow.

After a pause, she continued disjointedly. "Last winter, I was sick for more than a month. I decided to write to Sanxi . . . to have him come back . . . but Yuxiu was afraid Sanxi might get behind in his work. The trip would cost a lot, too, so she never told Sanxi I was sick. She was about to have the baby then, and she was very heavy, but she still trudged here and there to get medicine and herbs for me. She fed me my food spoon by spoon . . . . She carried bedpans for me . . . . Your auntie never had a daughter in her whole life, but could my own daughter have done more for me than that? So now, the more she does for me, the worse it makes me feel."

Aunt Liang kept wiping her eyes with the front of her cloak. I found my heart aching. After a good while, she looked up at Director and me. "Yuxiu is only twenty-four, now. I am not feudal-minded.

What's more, Sanxi had said that if . . . Yuxiu should . . . . But as her mother-in-law I'm too embarrassed to bring it up with her. You comrades who go out in the world understand these things better than I do. Won't you please help me persuade her to . . . find a proper man . . . . "

"Mom! You . . . . " Yuxiu burst into the room and knelt down before Aunt Liang. She covered her mother-in-law's mouth with one hand and wept. "Mom! Don't talk like that. I'll take care of you forever."

Aunt Liang held her daughter-in-law tightly in her arms. "Xiu, no . . . . Sooner or later I would have to come right out and . . . tell you. I thought . . . the sooner I told you . . . the better."

"Mom!" Yuxiu covered her mother-in-law's mouth again, her head nestled close against Aunt Liang. She was weeping uncontrollably.

"Go on and cry, Xiu. Cry it all out . . . all the tears that you've been holding back." Aunt Liang was shedding tears, too. She stroked her daughter-in-law's hair. "A good cry will make you feel better."

Yuxiu at once stopped wailing, but continued to sob.

Unable to bear the sight of it, Director had turned his back to them, his notebook and pen lying on the floor. I buried my face in my hands. I could feel tears streaming down through my fingers.

The kitchen police supervisor had learned three days before that Aunt Liang and her family would soon be leaving. He got a ride into town on the regiment quartermaster's truck when it went for provisions, and he bought a whole lot of dried shrimp, sea cucumber, tree fungus, frozen prawns . . . food that the soldiers would not get to eat even on festival days. He was set to cook a big farewell meal for Aunt Liang and her family.

Yes. Auntie and Yuxiu were certainly entitled to a feast; they deserved to enjoy all the delicacies in the world.

The next morning, the regiment sent a jeep to Company Nine to wait for the Liangs to get ready and then drive them to the railway station.

The battalion commander arrived. My mother arrived. Each squad sent a representative to be at the meal for Aunt Liang and her family.

More than twenty dishes were laid on the table. The kitchen police supervisor had said that jiaozi brings good luck to people starting a trip, so he had made a lot of jiaozi, too.

My mother held Panpan in her arms and fed her a bottle of milk.

We kept picking up food and putting it into Aunt Liang's and Yuxiu's bowls, urging them to eat. We piled their bowls high with all kinds of food but neither woman touched her chopsticks.

Everyone knew that these dishes had not been prepared for us to enjoy, but for the Liang family. However, urging the Liangs to enjoy the food did make us all feel better about eating.

At the behest of everyone, Aunt Liang did eat two jiaozi and take two swallows of broth. Yuxiu took only one jiaozi and one swallow of broth; she said she never ate very much in the morning and that she was full.

The soldiers came to the company headquarters one by one to see the Liangs off. I had warned them the day before to hold back their tears until after Aunt Liang and her family were gone.

Unexpectedly, Duan Yuguo started weeping. Then some of the other soldiers did too.

Aunt Liang stood up. "Don't cry . . . never cry. Us farmers may sweat a lot, or even get scratched up doing our farm work. But how are you going to defend our country without shedding some blood? Sanxi died for the country. He died a worthy death."

Hearing her words, Duan Yuguo started crying aloud, and others broke down, too. But someone gave Duan Yuguo a nudge and he stopped. The others also became aware of the unseemliness of crying in front of Aunt Liang and Yuxiu. The room soon quieted down.

"Xiu, it's not early. Let's not bother the comrades anymore. We should go now." Aunt Liang paused, then she said to Yuxiu, "Xiu, fetch me those scissors."

Xiu took out a pair of pinking shears wrapped in a bundle of blue and white cloth and handed them to Aunt Liang. Aunt Liang felt along the hem of her cloak. She located a bulge, picked up the scissors, and cut off the bulge with a few snips.

We all watched silently, not knowing what she was doing.

With her bony hand, Aunt Liang pulled out a wad of new *renminbi* notes from the opening in her cloak and laid them out on the table. The thick wad of ten-yuan notes was tied with a flame-red strip of silk cloth. Then she searched for another bulge in the hem of her cloak and brought out a wad of old *renminbi*, also all in ten-yuan notes.

I was stupefied! What could she be going to do with the money? The three generations had walked here step by step more than 160 li from the railway station in order to save the bus fare, and all the while Aunt Liang had this much money with her!

Aunt Liang took a look at me and then pointed at the two wads of money on the table. "That is 550 kuai and this is 70 kuai."

Yuxiu passed a small piece of paper to me. "Instructor, may I give the note to you and trust you to take care of this for us?"

I took the note and saw that it was the list of debts that Liang Sanxi had written down and left with his family! The paper was the same as that of Liang Sanxi's blood-stained list. In fact, it was the other half of the same piece of paper, torn from a small note pad.

I felt a sudden tingling in my scalp.

Aunt Liang said calmly, "Sanxi's last words to me were to have Yuxiu and me repay his debts of 620 yuan. Xiu, show them Sanxi's letter."

Yuxiu handed me a letter.

Finally! We had found the martyr Liang Sanxi's last letter. It read

Dear Yuxiu,

How are you? Is Mom still going strong?

I got your letter yesterday, so now I know how you are doing. It took a month for your letter to get here because it went to Shandong and the troops in the rear office forwarded it to me.

You said in your letter that you were going to have our baby at any time, so it must be almost a month old now. I bless you from thousands of li away. I wish you and the baby well. I'm sure Mom grinned from ear to ear when she saw her grandson—or granddaughter—come into the world.

Xiu, I know that I have been promising you since last June to come home on furlough soon, and that you have longed for my return day after day. However, for a variety of reasons, it's a month into the next year and I still haven't been able to get back home. Although you never complained in your letters, I feel very guilty about it from the bottom of my heart.

In my last letter of a month ago I told you that our company was going out to perform a task. I didn't say anything about it in detail. But now I can tell you that our company has left its original position and moved by train to the international border in Yunnan. Here we saw for ourselves the belligerent tactics of the Vietnamese devils. They invaded our territory whenever they felt like it, and slaughtered our citizens! As a nation that had just ended ten years of turmoil, we were hardly in a good position to expend more manpower and material resources on warfare. But this is a war we have to fight! Anybody who came here and saw what was happening would think we would shame the Chinese people if we didn't fight back against those small-time Vietnamese overlords—not to mention what our servicemen would think.

By the time you read this letter, I will be fighting in a counterattack on the battlefield.

Xiu, we were both born in the mountain village of Date Blossom Valley. You are eight years younger than I. We grew up together. We've never had a fight since the day we fell in love and got married, except once. You probably remember it very well. It was when you came to see me at my outfit last March. I made a joke, saying that someday I'd probably go to the front and get hit by a bullet. I didn't think this would upset you so much, but you thumped my chest with your fist and said I was bad, that I had a hard heart. Then you wept, wept with such grief. I did my best to soothe you. You asked if I would ever say such words again. I said "no," and you stopped crying. You said, "Neither of us should die first. If we have to die, we'll die together." Xiu, I know you love me, with so much selflessness and purity, with all your heart.

However, there are soldiers because there are wars. There wouldn't be any army otherwise. Xiu, I am not joking this time. I have to tell you: this may be the last letter that I write to you.

We have been married for almost three years, Xiu, and during this time I've had two furloughs, including the one when I came home to get married and the time when you visited my army unit. All told, we have lived together less than ninety days! The last night, before you went back home, you cried all night long. Now, I think it was very likely the last time that we'll see each other. I knew you didn't want to leave me, and I truly wished you could have stayed with me longer, too. But you were concerned about Mom being at home alone, and about getting the farm work done. You got on the train but you kept turning back your tearful face. My heart broke then. "Hardship is different from pain," as they say. For an officer at the company level, the most painful thing is the long-term separation—husband and wife longing for each other from afar. I had thought about getting transferred to civilian work back in Date Blossom Valley. I'd never regret losing this salary—it hardly covered the money we spent on travel. Although life in the countryside is hard, at least we would be together and could share our problems. That would be the best of all. But, thinking it over again, what would happen if nobody served as company officers? The soldiers need someone to lead. The border must have people to guard it. The country must have people to defend it.

Xiu, I came into this world without a stitch of clothes, and grew up sucking the milk of a peasant mother. Compared to the others, I—the bumpkin company commander—really am a nobody. But I often think of myself as luckier than other people. I really have been lucky. And I feel this way because of you: my dear Xiu. I am so pleased whenever I hear my comrades praise you. Not only am I pleased, but I am proud of you, too. However, it also fills my heart with grief when I think of you. Because of the misfortunes my family has suffered, and because of the poverty of our village, you can never have a well-to-do life with me. Even though our villagers address me as "Big Officer" and I have a monthly company-rank salary of 60 yuan, I have never bought you so much as a piece of ordinary clothing, not to mention woolens or nylons. But still you comfort me: "It's all right, as long as I have clothes to wear. We fall short of the best but we're better off than the worst." When I remember it now, Xiu, I don't know how to express my thanks to you. I can only say that I will never forget your graciousness and kindheartedness, not even after death.

Xiu, if I die on the battlefield, then the following words will be my last will:

I firmly believe that after my death you and Mom, as people from the old revolutionary base area, should never bother my superiors or comrades. Mom has done her bit for the revolution. I'm her only son, so once I am dead, the government will make the appropriate arrangements and take good care of her. She'll be secure for the rest of her life. I expect you to receive the martyr's family's pension, to the extent provided in the government regulations only, and never ask the superiors for more. We may be poor, but we are no lower than anyone else in spirit. Besides that, our country is not rich, and we should think about our country's difficulties. It's true that during the ten years of turmoil quite a few people abused their power and influence to line their pockets but, although those people are still around, we must never follow the example of people who are utterly devoid of any conscience. An individual without even a grain of patriotism is unworthy to be human.

Xiu, when you came to my company last year, you knew I had debts of about 800 yuan. I still owe my comrades 620 yuan. I'm enclosing a list of my debts. I had hoped to pay off the debts in three or four years by cutting back on expenses as much as possible. Then life would be much easier for us. This plan will come to nothing if I die. But don't worry. According to the regulations, a serviceman's family can get a pension if he dies. It would be 500 yuan for a soldier, 550 yuan for a company or platoon-rank officer. After you draw the 550 yuan from the Civil Administration Department, the other 70 yuan you'll need to pay off the debt will be easy to find. Could you sell the pig you've raised? Anyway, you must pay off all my debts when you and Mom come to my company. Those comrades who lent me the money are either my close superiors or my best friends in the army, and their families are not rich, either. If anyone named on the list dies too, I want you to ask one of the comrades in my company to pass the money on to his family. This debt can never die, even if the creditor dies. Be sure to remember this!

Xiu, there is one more thing to discuss that is even more important than the debts. I hope you will faithfully follow my instructions. I have been thinking it over these past few days. Why do we shed blood on the battlefield?—so our people can live a better life. "The people" certainly includes you—my beloved wife. Xiu, you are only twenty-four, in the flower of life. Not only do I hope that you live on courageously after my death, but I also hope you can have a happy life. Our village is backward in education, but you graduated from junior middle school. I hope you will have the courage to ignore those old, feudal ideas, such as "a woman of virtue would never marry two men." You must firmly break away from those customs and marry again when you meet the proper man. Mom is a sensible person. I believe that she wouldn't try to stop you—she wouldn't want to. Please be mindful of this! Otherwise, my soul will never rest in peace.

Xiu, I leave you almost nothing except the list of debts. I wore out all my uniforms in military training. I have one uniform overcoat that I've never worn since they issued it to me two years ago. I've kept it in a plastic bag. My comrades will pass it along to you after my death. Then you could make a present of the new overcoat to your future husband.

Xiu, our company is a full-time military training outfit. I've heard that we will be assigned the toughest job. It is quite possible that we will part forever. So I want to say good-bye to you.

You had asked me in your letter to give a name to our baby. Whether it is a boy or a girl, let's call him (or her) "Panpan," to express our hope for the future. Now that the "Gang of Four" has been smashed, and the Eleventh National Congress of the Party has just convened, we are seeing the dawn of a magnificent future. There is hope for us, and there is hope for all the peasants.

I reckon that you delivered a month ago and I'm just now able to mail this letter. I haven't been there to help during your lying-in. Please kiss him (her) for me, my little Panpan that I have never seen.

With best wishes.

Sanxi
Jan. 28, 1979

I could not help bursting into tears when I read the letter. I wailed.

I took up the 550 yuan pension and cried to Aunt Liang, "Auntie, my good Auntie! You . . . this pension . . . . No, you can't . . . . "

Now everybody present understood what had happened. The room was full of sobs.

Duan Yuguo, still crying, ran out to bring back his pocket radio, and then took off his electronic watch. He banged them on the table. "Our commander's debts . . . we shall pay them off!"

"We shall pay them off!" the other three of us affirmed. Tears blurred my sight. I could no longer tell who was who. I only saw watches coming off one by one, and wad after wad of banknotes, all piled up on the table in front of me.

When the heartbreaking sobs had died down, I begged Aunt Liang in a choked voice, "Auntie, I . . . I was brought up by your milk . . . . Please allow me to . . . to pay off my brother Sanxi's debts."

Aunt Liang wiped her eyes with the back of her hand. Her old voice also became hoarse. "My children, Yuxiu and I . . . we're obliged to you for your . . . kindness, much obliged. But Sanxi has left his last will . . . words that I can't disobey. Otherwise, he would never rest in peace."

No matter how we implored her, Auntie would only repeat that the last words of the dead must never be violated. She laid down the 620 yuan and got into the jeep with Yuxiu.

My mother had collapsed from so much grief, and couldn't accompany Aunt Liang and her family to the railway station. I, faltering as I walked, was helped into the jeep by the soldiers.

They rode away: the three generations from Yimeng Mountain then rode away.

Epilogue

Zhao Mengsheng's story touched me so much that both of us sobbed without saying anything.

After a long silence, Zhao Mengsheng rubbed his eyes and said to me in a husky voice, "This is why I have treated Aunt Liang as my own mother during the past three years. Every month, as soon as I'm paid, the first thing I do is write a letter to ask her how she is and send her thirty yuan. Of course, I could afford to send her a hundred, or hundreds of yuan all at once, but I wouldn't do that. I know that Aunt Liang doesn't care about money. It's my way of comforting her and reminding her now and then that a son of hers stands guard on the border; that he was brought up on her milk, and that he still believes in fulfilling his responsibilities as a son. But now, she . . . . " Zhao Mengsheng picked up the money order for 1,200 yuan and slapped his head. "Why? Why did Auntie send all the money back? Doesn't she need money for everyday things? Of course she does."

Duan Yuguo gazed at me and said softly, "Last spring, when I was a copy clerk at Company Nine, I was selected to represent the Company and make a special trip with Instructor to go and visit Aunt Liang and her family in the Yimeng Mountains. Agricultural production had gone over to the Responsibility System, and some restrictions on economic policy had been relaxed. The Liangs didn't have to worry about food, and they were wearing better clothes. However, Instructor and I both noticed that their rolled bed mat had been patched with blue cloth in more than ten places. Auntie and Yuxiu wouldn't even spend money on a new bed mat."

"Why? Why was that?" Zhao Mengsheng became introspective. "Does she still blame me and think I'm unworthy to care for her? No, never! I haven't hidden a thing from her these past three years."

"No, it couldn't possibly be that," Secretary Duan Yuguo said to Zhao Mengsheng. Then he turned to me. "Lao Li, you ought to go and interview Aunt Liang when you get back to Shandong. Aunt Liang really is a kindhearted person. Last spring, when Instructor and I went to see her in the Yimeng Mountains, she treated us very well. She racked her brains finding things to entertain us. She quietly slaughtered two hens she had been keeping—and they were still laying eggs. We would have stayed a few days longer but didn't for fear we would tire her out."

Zhao Mengsheng asked, "Xiao Duan, why do you think Auntie sent back all of the money? Please help me out."

Duan Yuguo blinked his long eyelashes. "I was reading a novel recently, and the hero said, 'Living on charity will make one humble, and the most painful thing is being pitied.' Aunt Liang and Yuxiu are people of much character. Maybe . . . . "

"What?!" Zhao Mengsheng sprung to his feet and seized Duan Yuguo by the lapels. "You petty intellectual, what did you just say?! You . . . you . . . . "

Face to face with his political instructor, who was suddenly raving with fury, Duan Yuguo became tongue-tied. "Instructor, I . . . I . . . ."

Zhao Mengsheng loosened his grasp, still red with anger. "Charity? Pity? Forget about me! Does anybody—I want to ask out loud!—does anybody have the right to pity Aunt Liang? Is anybody qualified to pity Aunt Liang? It absolutely stands to reason that she should live a better life. *She* has the right and qualifications to enjoy her remaining years!"

Finishing these words, Zhao Mengsheng sank into the chair with his forehead cupped in his hands. He became painfully silent again.

Duan Yuguo hung his head and said with self-reproach, "Instructor, I . . . I was wrong."

Long after dinnertime, the courier came by to deliver a few newspapers and a letter to Zhao Mengsheng. He also urged us to go and eat dinner.

Zhao Mengsheng opened the envelope. After looking over the letter, he passed it to me. "You can take a look at this."

The letter was from Wu Shuang, Zhao Mengsheng's mother. The point of it was that the reason Liu Lan had overstayed her leave was that she really was ill. She had acute pneumonia, and had been in the hospital for twenty days. Wu Shuang stated in the letter that Liu Lan had never deceived the Party by getting a doctor's certificate of illness through a backdoor deal. As a mother and a Party member, Wu Shuang wanted to certify Liu Lan's innocence. She wrote that Liu Lan had recovered from her illness and would soon be returning to the front. But she added that Liu Lan still had serious ideological problems: she was determined to get herself transferred back to the city and out of uniform. However, Wu Shuang hoped that her son would show more patience in reasoning with Liu Lan. Foaming with rage would solve nothing, she wrote. She also told Zhao Mengsheng that she had just completed the formalities for retirement and would soon be leaving for the Yimeng Mountains to visit Aunt Liang and her family.

Seeing that I had finished the letter, Zhao Mengsheng said, "Last summer, when Liu Lan graduated from the Army Medical University, she was bent on getting herself assigned to the city where her parents lived. I argued with her, over and over again, until we were almost ready to divorce. But she finally did come to this border outpost, quite unwillingly. Mother played an active role in it, too. She had blocked all the back doors that Liu Lan might have slipped through. Maybe I carried it too far. I'm only human myself. It wasn't only Liu Lan; I too have wavered and hesitated these years about whether or not to transfer from the army and work in the city. It's just that whenever I think of the martyrs, of Aunt Liang and her family, I feel ashamed of myself. Persuading Liu Lan to stay here, though, will be much more difficult."

I stayed overnight at the battalion headquarters. Only a small brook separated Company Nine's barracks from the battalion headquarters. The next day, Zhao Mengsheng led me to Company Nine.

I held a briefing at Company Nine in the morning. In the afternoon, the whole company came out to collect flowers, and I joined in.

Tomorrow would be Qing Ming—the Day of Pure Brightness. The soldiers of Company Nine were to tie up some wreaths with the flowers that had been gathered and place them in front of the martyrs' graves.

Flowers blossom all the year 'round in the Yunnan border region, but they are at their height of profusion during Qing Ming. Up and down the mountains, along roadsides and the banks of streams, flowers had come into bloom everywhere. Their redolence sweetened the spring breeze. By dusk, the soldiers who had been collecting flowers gathered on the bank of the brook next to Company Nine.

The red glow of the sunset shone brightly on the clear brook water that flowed from the distant mountains. The soldiers sat down beside the gentle waters and began to braid multicolored wreaths, one after another, using flame red cotton tree blossoms, golden pagoda tree flowers, pure white camellia, sky blue azalea, and all sorts of wildflowers. Then they took the wreaths to the brook and bathed them with water that splashed upon them in drops like pearls.

Duan Yuguo ran up to us all the way from the battalion headquarters and said to Zhao Mengsheng, "Instructor, here it is— Aunt Liang's letter! I have read it. That money order . . . oh, well, let Lao Li read it first!"

I took the letter and began to read

Mengsheng,

How are you? And how are the comrades?

I usually get Yuxiu to write for me when I answer your letters. But this time the letter's about Yuxiu, so I asked Teacher Sun of our village school to do the writing.

Two days ago I had someone go to the post office and send you back all the money you had been sending me for the past three years. It came to 1,200 yuan. Did you get it?

Everybody in our village likes you, Mengsheng. They say you are a good person and you didn't forget your old auntie. I hope you don't mind about me sending the money back. I'll tell you why I did it.

First, we really do have a better life now. Yuxiu, Panpan, and I each get a five-yuan pension. That comes to fifteen yuan every month. All the farmable land in the countryside has been contracted out to people on the

Responsibility System. The land gives a good yield. What's more, the people in our village got together and agreed to give preferential treatment to soldiers' families. The land that our family contracted is always the first to be plowed, and our crops are the first ones to get harvested, even before Yuxiu and I get down to work. This is one of the wonderful traditions of our area, which was one of the first to be liberated. Why, your old auntie has even paid off all her debts, and I lend a few yuan to my neighbors if they get into a bind.

The second thing is that the borders still aren't secure yet. It's not easy to stand guard out there in the wind and the rain. When Sanxi was the company commander, he told me that a lot of soldiers in his company were bad off when it came to money. When anybody in their family got sick or met a hardship, it would worry him to death. Sanxi would have helped them if he hadn't been so short on money himself. Anyway, I thought it over for a long time and I decided to send you back all the money that you mailed to me over the past three years. I just think it would be better to spend that money on soldiers who can't make ends meet, so they can protect our country and not have to worry about how the family's doing at home.

Mengsheng, now don't you send me any more money after this. It'll mean the world to me just to know that you still think of me as your auntie.

I also got that picture of Liu Lan that I asked you for last year. Isn't she a pretty girl! You said she couldn't bear her work on the front. Well, I don't agree with the way you complained about her. I can't stand by while you tear her down like that. A woman's not the same as a man. And don't you make her stand guard at night! Why, even our Yuxiu said she was afraid at night when she lived in the deep forest, not to mention a girl that grew up in the city. I want you to promise to take my advice.

I've come onto the most wonderful news lately. It's about Yuxiu. There is a schoolteacher named Xiao Chen in our village, and he's the same age as Yuxiu. Both of Xiao Chen's parents died two years ago, and he's never been married. He's an honest man, and handsome, too. We all think he's a good match for Yuxiu. Our villagers volunteered to be their matchmakers. Xiao Chen doesn't have any objection to it. He even offered to come to our home and take care of me. But I'm afraid that Yuxiu still has Sanxi in her heart and she won't go along with a marriage. As luck would have it, your mother wrote to me and said that she had retired from the service and was coming to see me. I hate to see your mother spend the money on the trip, *but now I'll be glad to see her. She can turn Yuxiu around. Then, whether Yuxiu nods her approval or not, your mother and I will be only too happy to arrange the wedding for them.*

After that, your auntie will have nothing left on her mind. Nothing.

With an olive cloud across its top, the rising sun revealed a tender smile. The rose-colored rays cast their hues upon green mountains and blue rivers.

All the members of Company Nine—as well as myself—led by Zhao Mengsheng, carried the wreaths of braided, fresh flowers slowly toward the cemetery of the martyrs.

We placed the wreaths one by one in front of the martyrs' graves.

Pine and cypress surrounded the cemetery; inside, meticulously cultivated flowering shrubs grew everywhere. Bouquets of canna bloomed luxuriantly in front of the grave of Liang Sanxi, the huge green leaves sending up spikes of spectacular flowers. The morning dewdrops rolled along the petals like shining pearls. Alongside Liang Sanxi's grave were the graves of Jin Kailai, vice-commander of Company Nine; Lei Kaihua "Beijing," the soldier of the 8.2 recoilless cannon squad; and Jin Xiaozhu, the bugler who was not quite seventeen.

Standing silently in front of the flowered graves, I suddenly felt that the most splendid jewelry, the most magnificent colors in the world, had all been assembled at the foot of this lofty mountain.

Translator's Note

Li Cunbao's novel, *The Wreath at the Foot of the Mountain*, became a sensation as soon as it was published in China late in 1982. Readers among the intelligentsia and progressive Party members were exhilarated by the sheer audacity of a novelist who dared to discuss openly the corruption of Party members and their hated "backdoor" system of influence-mongering. The belief at the language institute where my wife and I taught English at the time was that the old cadres had tried to abort publication of this novel but had been overridden by more pragmatic heads in the top leadership of China. Since 1982, the novel has been adapted into a Chinese movie, a stage play, and numerous locally produced operatic versions.

Chinese reviewers of *The Wreath* typically praised the novel, not so much for its exposé of corruption in high places, but because it made them weep. Whether or not Western readers succumb to the weighty emotionalism of the story, they are certain to be fascinated by the steady stream of details of the everyday life in a country where 800 million persons still live in the countryside.

The Wreath at the Foot of the Mountain will, I suspect, accomplish two paradoxical ends for the Western reader. It will disperse some of the mystery that obscures our understanding of the exotic, "inscrutable" Chinese. It will also leave it to readers to explain to themselves why Chinese officers were shown the restricted movie *Patton* as a morale booster before a military raid into the northern territory of their erstwhile ally, Vietnam.

Our goal during the translation of this novel was to present an edition that remains as true as possible to the substance and the spirit of the original. We took considerable care to sustain a natural reading experience. Chinese slang and dialect, which occur throughout the novel, have been rendered in American English equivalents wherever possible. Nevertheless, we feel that this translation faithfully preserves much of the texture and color of Li Cunbao's style.

Inevitably, the translators had to address numerous small items that are not explained in the text because their significance is obvious to Chinese readers. We have tried to make the text as accessible to Westerners as possible. A few terms, however, might bear some comment.

- The "ten years of turmoil" refers to the Cultural Revolution period, 1966 to 1976.
- The monetary system consists of three denominations: *fen*, *jiao*, and *yuan*. The last two terms are not ordinarily used in conversation, but are replaced with *mao* and *kuai*. The common currency of China is referred to as *renminbi*.
- Ordinary terms of address in Chinese are uncomplicated. One's occupation may serve as a term of address: Instructor Wang. Close friends may address each other as family members: Sister Wu, Aunt Liang. The respectful term *lao*, "old," is reserved for persons generally above the age of 40: Lao Zhao. *Xiao*, "little," denotes a younger person: Xiao Jin. The family name in Chinese precedes the given name.
- Private enterprise during the cultural revolution was severely constrained. Private plots of land, family-owned livestock, and free markets were all considered "capitalist tails" to be cut off. To be denied access to such enterprises was to be "bobtailed."
- Dazhai is a commune in Shanxi Province famous for its highly productive terraced fields. Mao Zedong exhorted citizens to "learn from Dazhai in agriculture." Mao's exhortations were not applied wisely in every case.
- *Jiaozi* are a staple of northern Chinese cuisine. For this dish, various meats, vegetables, and spices are minced, stuffed in rice flour wrappers, and boiled. They are similar to the wontons of Cantonese cooking, but plumper. The term is usually translated as "dumplings."
- Qing Ming literally means "pure bright." The Qing Ming celebration is an ancient ritual of paying respect to one's ancestors. It falls

on April 4 or 5.

A note on pronunciation may be helpful. The Roman characters used in the Pinyin transliteration system fairly well approximate the Chinese values with the following exceptions:

c = ts (but ch = ch)
g = the "hard" g in get
j = the English j
q = palatalized t
x = palatalized s
z = dz
zh = j made with the back of the tongue

James O. Belcher

Some Titles in the Series

JAMES J. WILHELM
General Editor

1. Lars Ahlin, *Cinnamoncandy*.
   Translated from Swedish by Hanna Kalter Weiss.

2. *Anthology of Belgian Symbolist Poets*.
   Translated from French by Donald F. Friedman.

3. Ariosto, *Five Cantos*.
   Translated from Italian by Leslie Z. Morgan.

4. *Kassia: The Legend, the Woman, and Her Work*.
   Translated from Greek by Antonia Tripolitis.

5. Antonio de Castro Alves, *The Major Abolitionist Poems*.
   Translated from Portuguese by Amy A. Peterson.

6. Li Cunbao, *The Wreath at the Foot of the Mountain*.
   Translated from Chinese by Chen Hanming and
   James O. Belcher.

7. Meïr Goldschmidt, *A Jew*.
   Translated from Danish by Kenneth Ober.

8. Árpád Göncz, *Plays and Other Writings*.
   Translated from Hungarian by Katharina and
   Christopher Wilson.

DATE DUE

Demco, Inc. 38-293